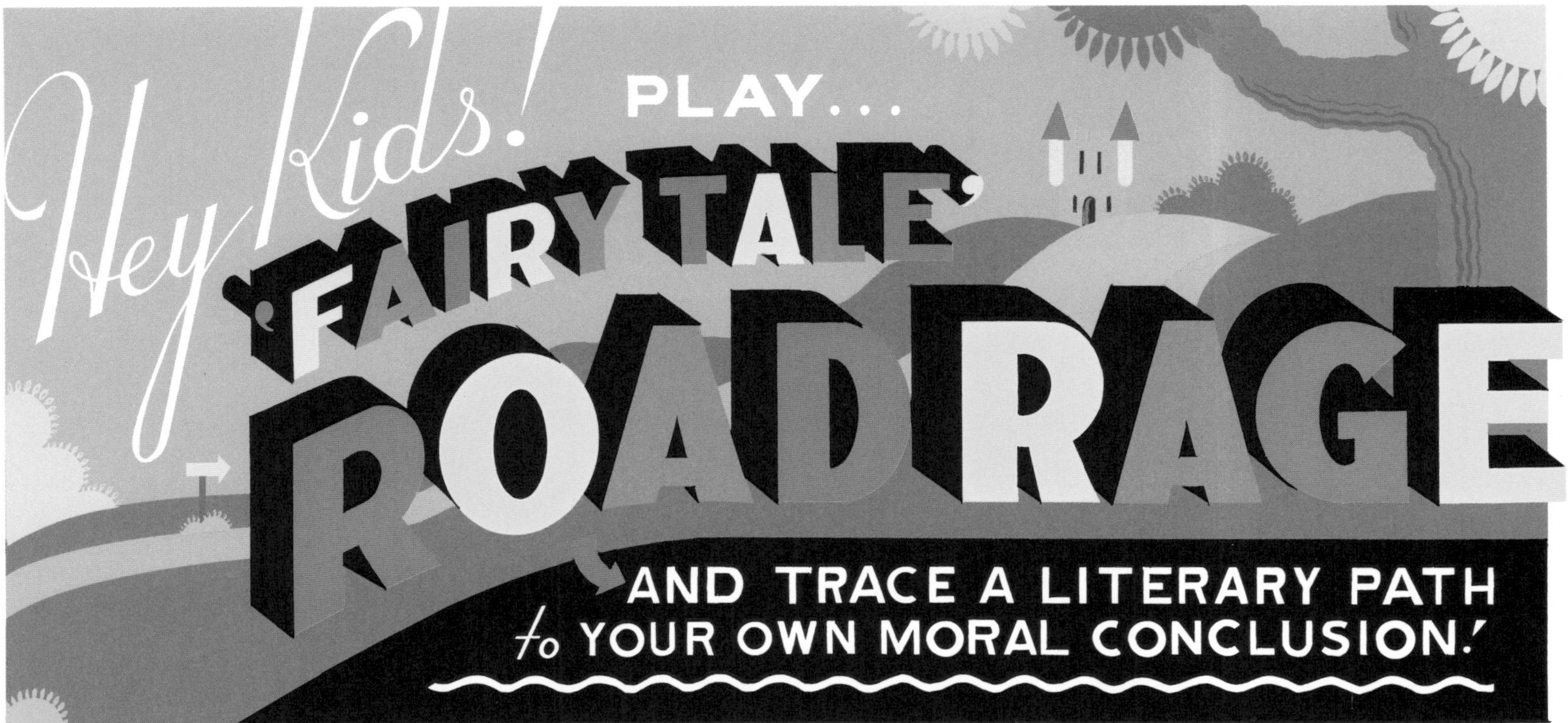
Hey Kids!
PLAY...
'FAIRY TALE'
ROAD RAGE
AND TRACE A LITERARY PATH
to YOUR OWN MORAL CONCLUSION!

featuring: **RUSTY BROWN** AND **CHALKY WHITE.**

'COLLECTEURS EXTRAORDINAIRE.'

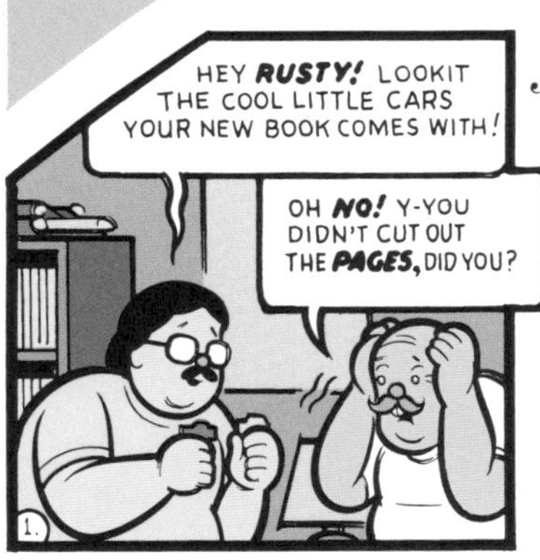
HEY RUSTY! LOOKIT THE COOL LITTLE CARS YOUR NEW BOOK COMES WITH!
OH NO! Y-YOU DIDN'T CUT OUT THE PAGES, DID YOU?
1.

INSTRUCTIONS.

(Grown-ups only.)

Buy book. Punch out chits. Make cars. Make die. Pick Frog, Grandma, Princess, or Wolf. Start on space marked "START." Roll die. Move cars around board. Colored chits match spaces on gameboard, and colored circles on storyboards. First to finish whole story wins.

INSTRUCTIONS. (Children only.)—The days of Fairy Tales are, alas, behind us, but the families and social classes which spawned them live on today in spanking new legacies and bloodlines. For example, the boy who sits behind you and pulls your hair in fifth period may be descended from a mutated brown slimetoad, or the girl who tries to hit you with the dodgeball every week in gym class may be the great-great-granddaughter of a bloated man-pig. Who knows? Who cares? Most people don't—and we really don't, either—but it makes a swell idea for a board game, and that's what we have here for you to try and puzzle out the next time Mom or Dad won't drive you to the video arcade.

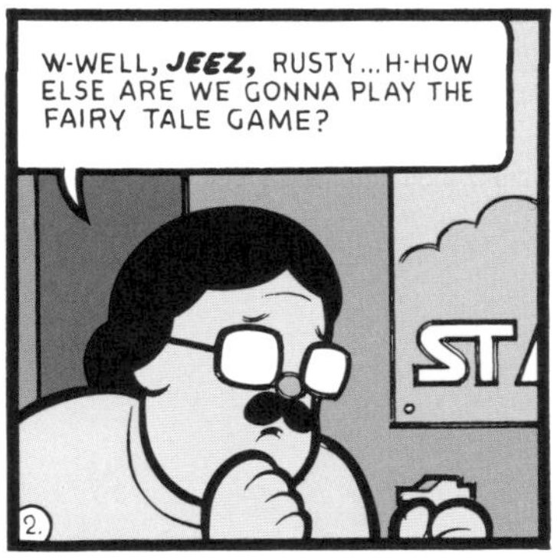
W-WELL, JEEZ, RUSTY...H-HOW ELSE ARE WE GONNA PLAY THE FAIRY TALE GAME?
2.

Object of the Game. — The object of the game is to be the first player to complete one "storyboard" of 9 empty spaces with 9 corresponding little circular "chits," which, when so arranged, will complete a story of amusing and rakish details—particularly if read aloud, and with dramatic relish.

Commencement of play. — This is a game for one to four players. Each player, upon the decision to engage in play, is issued a "storyboard" upon which is printed one of four characters: a Frog, a Princess, a Grandma, or a Wolf. The smart child will note that each storyboard is arrayed with a number of blank circles, and that these circles are colored in a corresponding manner with 70 little circular "chits," which should be punched out and spread out, facedown. The smarter child will note that the game board (see inside front cover of this book) is colored with an exactly matching assortment of shades, as well. The smartest of all children will then deduce that, due to the similarity of these colors, some sort of relationship exists between the playing pieces, the spaces on the board, and the spaces on the storyboards. This child should be immediately excused from play and be signed up for top-level government service, as he or she is obviously more gifted than the adults who currently hold such positions.

All circular pieces should be punched out, all four storyboards should be separated, all four playing pieces (the little cars at the front of this folio) assembled, and the "die" (singular for "dice") assembled. Each child should select the character he or she wants to be, and set the corresponding car at the spot marked "START" at the four corners of the gameboard. Then, all should breathe deeply, relax, and begin.

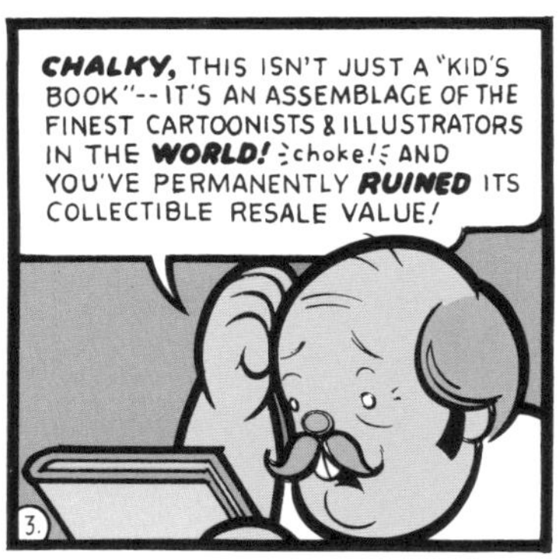
CHALKY, THIS ISN'T JUST A "KID'S BOOK"-- IT'S AN ASSEMBLAGE OF THE FINEST CARTOONISTS & ILLUSTRATORS IN THE WORLD! :choke!: AND YOU'VE PERMANENTLY RUINED ITS COLLECTIBLE RESALE VALUE!
3.

The highest roll of the die goes first; in case of a tie, continue to roll back and forth until a higher roll is made. In case of a four-way tie, begin again, draw lots, or simply go outside and play for a while, or ask your Mother or Father whom they prefer most.

Movement of pieces. — Movement is always *forward,* that is, not backward, or contrary to the direction embarked upon from the starting point. This rule is only broken if the player reaches a "dead end"—as in the less clean parts of Fairyland—and in such cases he or she is allowed to "back up" and then move on from that point. Movement corresponds exactly to the number of spaces indicated by the roll of the "die" (up to six spaces, should one choose to use a standardized die.)

Note: "Collectors" are "adults" who like to have "one of everything," or, specifically, items which they were denied as children. "Pristine" manufacturing condition and "original packaging" are of a premium to them, as are "rare" or "hard-to-find" items. You should, under all conditions, avoid growing up to be a "collector."

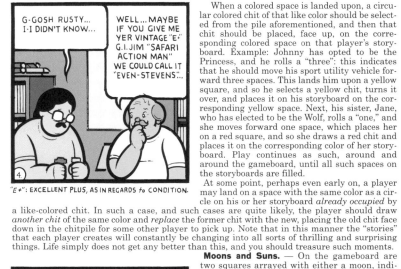

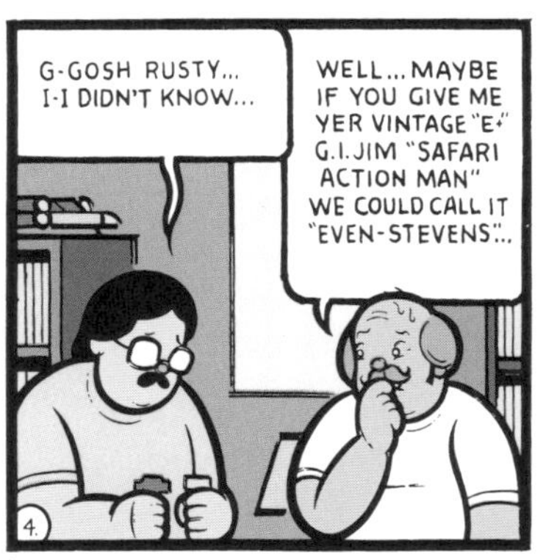
G-GOSH RUSTY... I-I DIDN'T KNOW...
WELL... MAYBE IF YOU GIVE ME YER VINTAGE "E+" G.I. JIM "SAFARI ACTION MAN" WE COULD CALL IT "EVEN-STEVENS"...
4.

"E+": EXCELLENT PLUS, AS IN REGARDS to CONDITION.

When a colored space is landed upon, a circular colored chit of that like color should be selected from the pile aforementioned, and then that chit should be placed, face up, on the corresponding colored space on that player's storyboard. Example: Johnny has opted to be the Princess, and he rolls a "three": this indicates that he should move his sport utility vehicle forward three spaces. This lands him upon a yellow square, and so he selects a yellow chit, turns it over, and places it on his storyboard on the corresponding yellow space. Next, his sister, Jane, who has elected to be the Wolf, rolls a "one," and she moves forward one space, which places her on a red square, and so she draws a red chit and places it on the corresponding color of her storyboard. Play continues as such, around and around the gameboard, until all such spaces on the storyboards are filled.

At some point, perhaps even early on, a player may land on a space with the same color as a circle on his or her storyboard *already occupied* by a like-colored chit. In such a case, and such cases are quite likely, the player should draw *another chit* of the same color and *replace* the former chit with the new, placing the old chit face down in the chitpile for some other player to pick up. Note that in this manner the "stories" that each player creates will constantly be changing into all sorts of thrilling and surprising things. Life simply does not get any better than this, and you should treasure such moments.

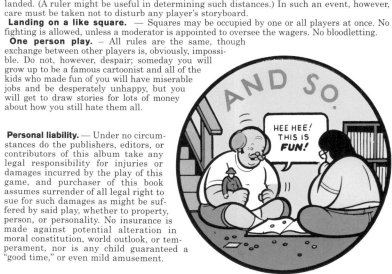

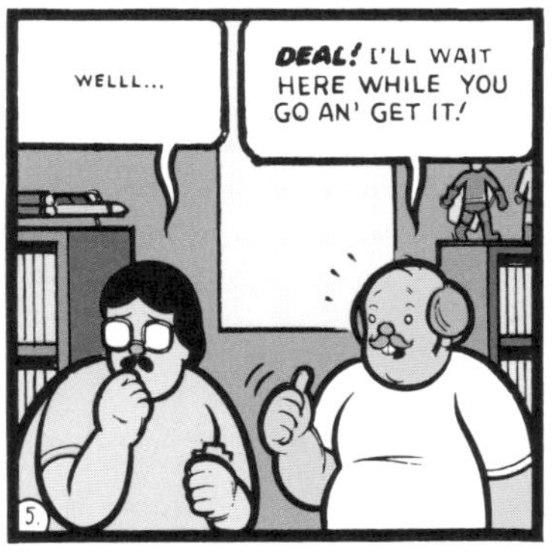
WELLL...
DEAL! I'LL WAIT HERE WHILE YOU GO AN' GET IT!
5.

Moons and Suns. — On the gameboard are two squares arrayed with either a moon, indicating skip one turn, or a sun, meaning take another turn. Strict adherence to these rules is demanded.

Special spaces. — There are also special spaces which instruct the player to "draw one chit of their choice" or "lose two chits"; in the case of a loss, the player removes the first chits in order from the storyboard, reading left to right.

Heisenberg Attack and Tornado. — Each of these spaces, when landed upon by a player, indicates a special sort of action. In the case of the "Heisenberg Attack," all players must switch characters, storyboards, and chits with the player to their immediate right; this is most effectively accomplished by simply getting up and changing seating places. The second circle, or "Tornado," instructs that the gameboard be thrown up in the air (by the player landing on this spot) and play restarted with each car placed upon the square nearest to where it landed. (A ruler might be useful in determining such distances.) In such an event, however, care must be taken not to disturb any player's storyboard.

Landing on a like square. — Squares may be occupied by one or all players at once. No fighting is allowed, unless a moderator is appointed to oversee the wagers. No bloodletting.

One person play. – All rules are the same, though exchange between other players is, obviously, impossible. Do not, however, despair; someday you will grow up to be a famous cartoonist and all of the kids who made fun of you will have miserable jobs and be desperately unhappy, but you will get to draw stories for lots of money about how you still hate them all.

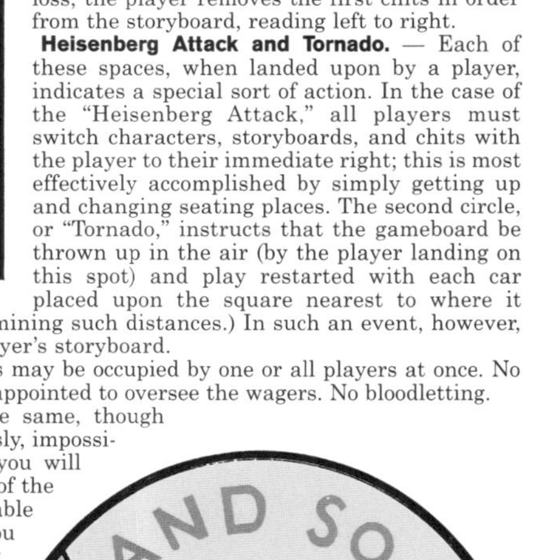
AND SO.
HEE HEE! THIS IS FUN!

Personal liability. — Under no circumstances do the publishers, editors, or contributors of this album take any legal responsibility for injuries or damages incurred by the play of this game, and purchaser of this book assumes surrender of all legal right to sue for such damages as might be suffered by said play, whether to property, person, or personality. No insurance is made against potential alteration in moral constitution, world outlook, or temperament, nor is any child guaranteed a "good time," or even mild amusement.

Little Lit

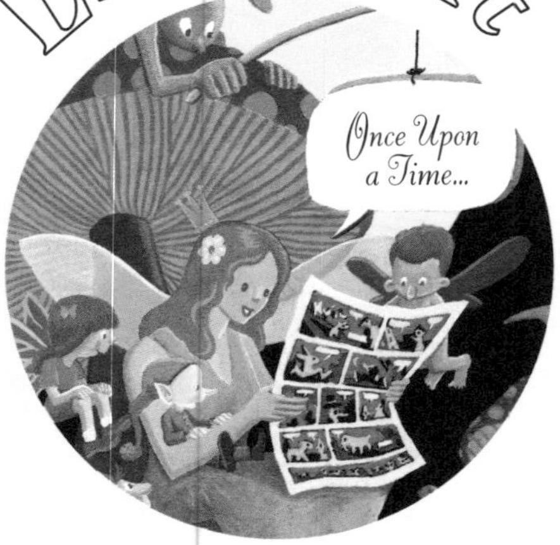
Once Upon a Time...

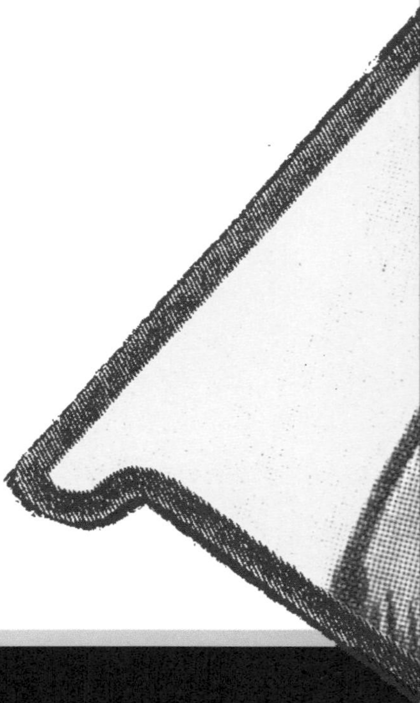

Folklore & Fairy Tale Funnies

designed by CHIP KIDD and ART SPIEGELMAN

dedicated to NADJA and DASHIELL

editorial associates:
NOVA REN SUMA
R. SIKORYAK

assistants
MARIKO KAWAGUCHI
DAN NADEL

with thanks to:
GREG CAPTAIN
JOHN KURAMOTO
IAIN MURRAY

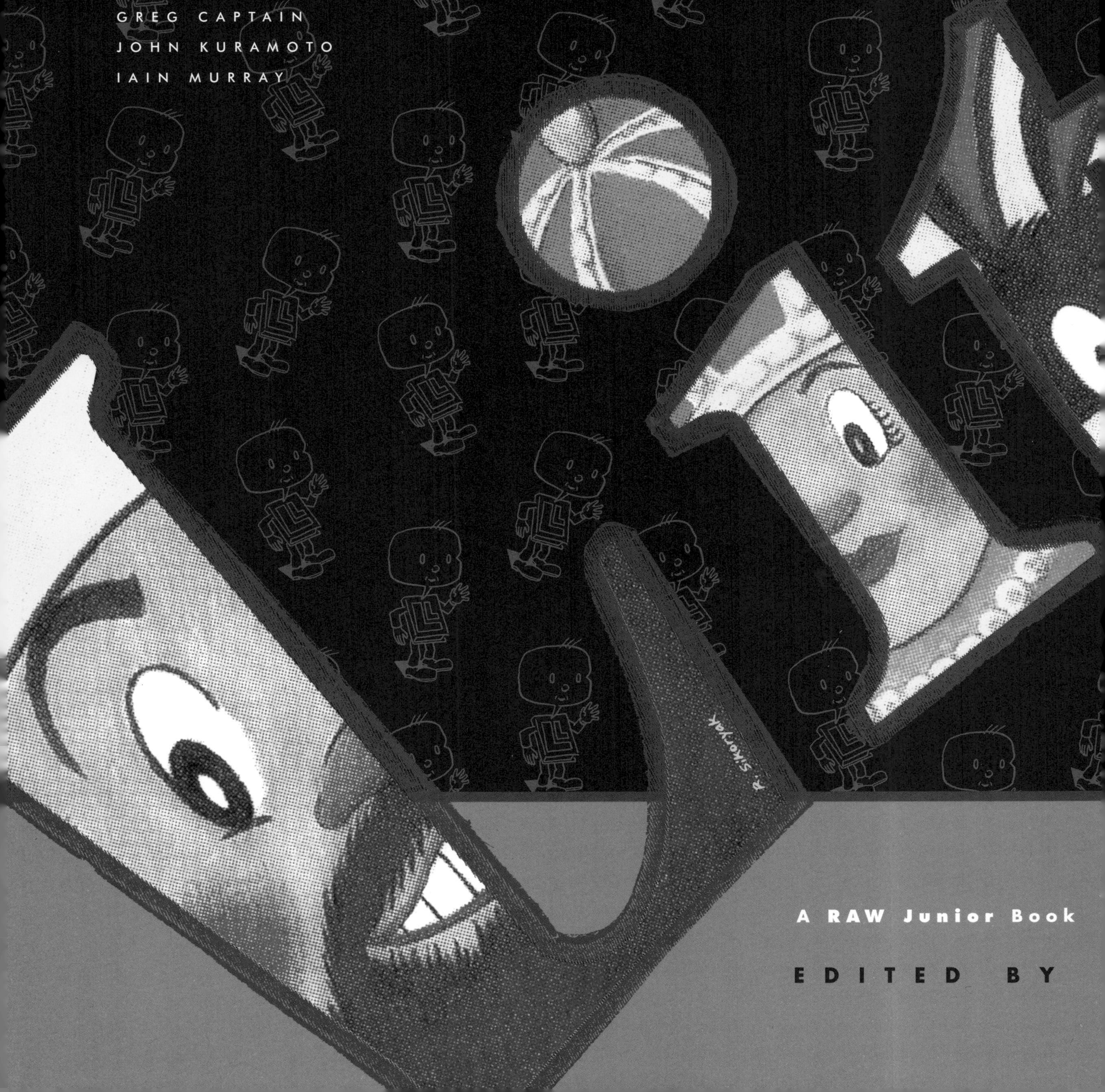
R. Sikoryak

A RAW Junior Book

EDITED BY

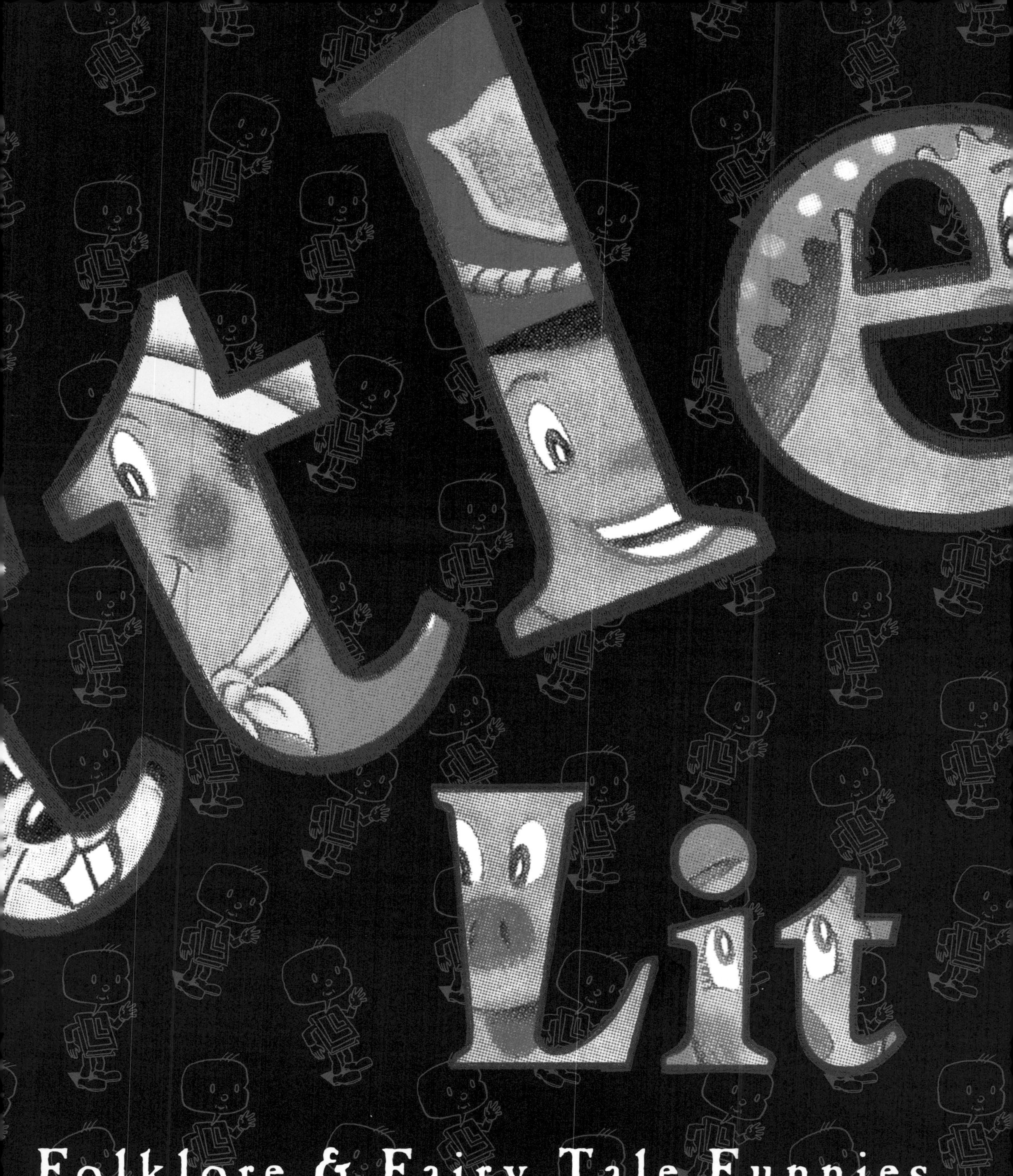
Lit

Folklore & Fairy Tale Funnies

with **JOANNA COTLER BOOKS**/an imprint of HarperCollins*Publishers*

ART SPIEGELMAN & FRANÇOISE MOULY

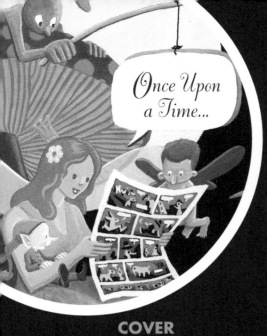

Once Upon a Time...

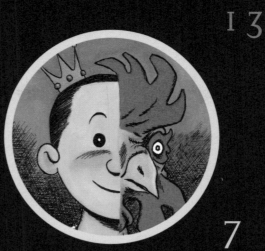
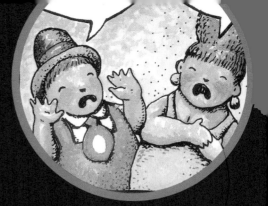
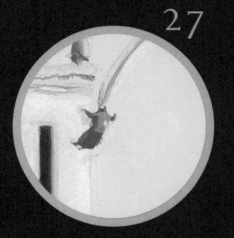
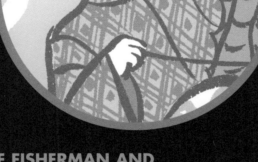
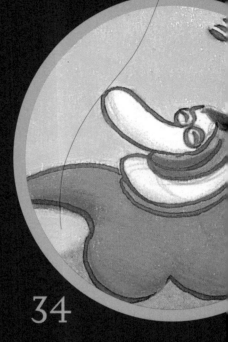
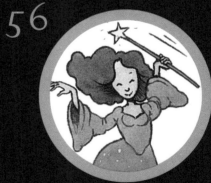
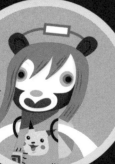
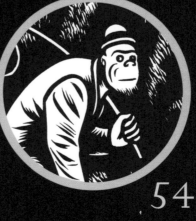
C   N   T   E

N T S

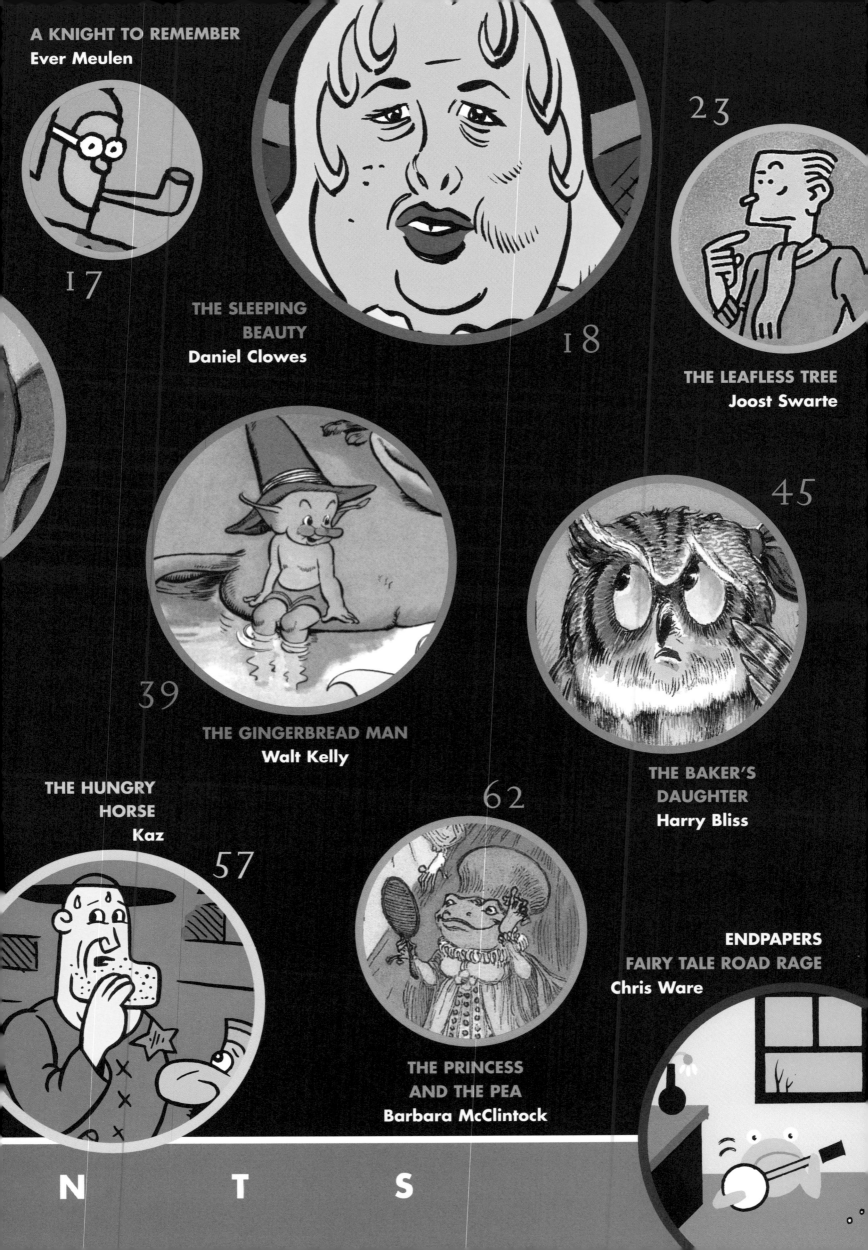

C o p y r i g h t
© 2000 by RAW Junior, LLC, 27 Greene Street, New
York, NY 10013. All rights reserved. No part of this book
may be used or reproduced in any manner whatsoever without written
permission except in the case of brief quotations embodied in critical
articles and reviews. Little Lit is a trademark of RAW Junior, LLC. For infor-
mation write to HarperCollins Children's Books, a division of HarperCollins
Publishers Inc., 1350 Avenue of the Americas, New York, NY 10019.
www.harperchildrens.com. Library of Congress Cataloging-in-
Publication Data: LITTLE LIT: Folklore & Fairy Tale Funnies/edited by Art
Spiegelman & Françoise Mouly. p.cm.– (Little Lit ;1) "A RAW Junior book with
Joanna Cotler books." ISBN 0-06-028624-5 I. Title: Little Lit: Folklore & Fairy
Tale Funnies. II. Spiegelman, Art. III. Mouly, Françoise. IV. Series.
PN6727.S6F65 2000 741.5 ' 9—dc21   99-51484.
Printed in China by Oceanic Graphic Printing.
10 9 8
7 6 5
4 3
2
1

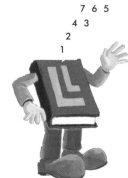

Visit us at www.little-lit.com

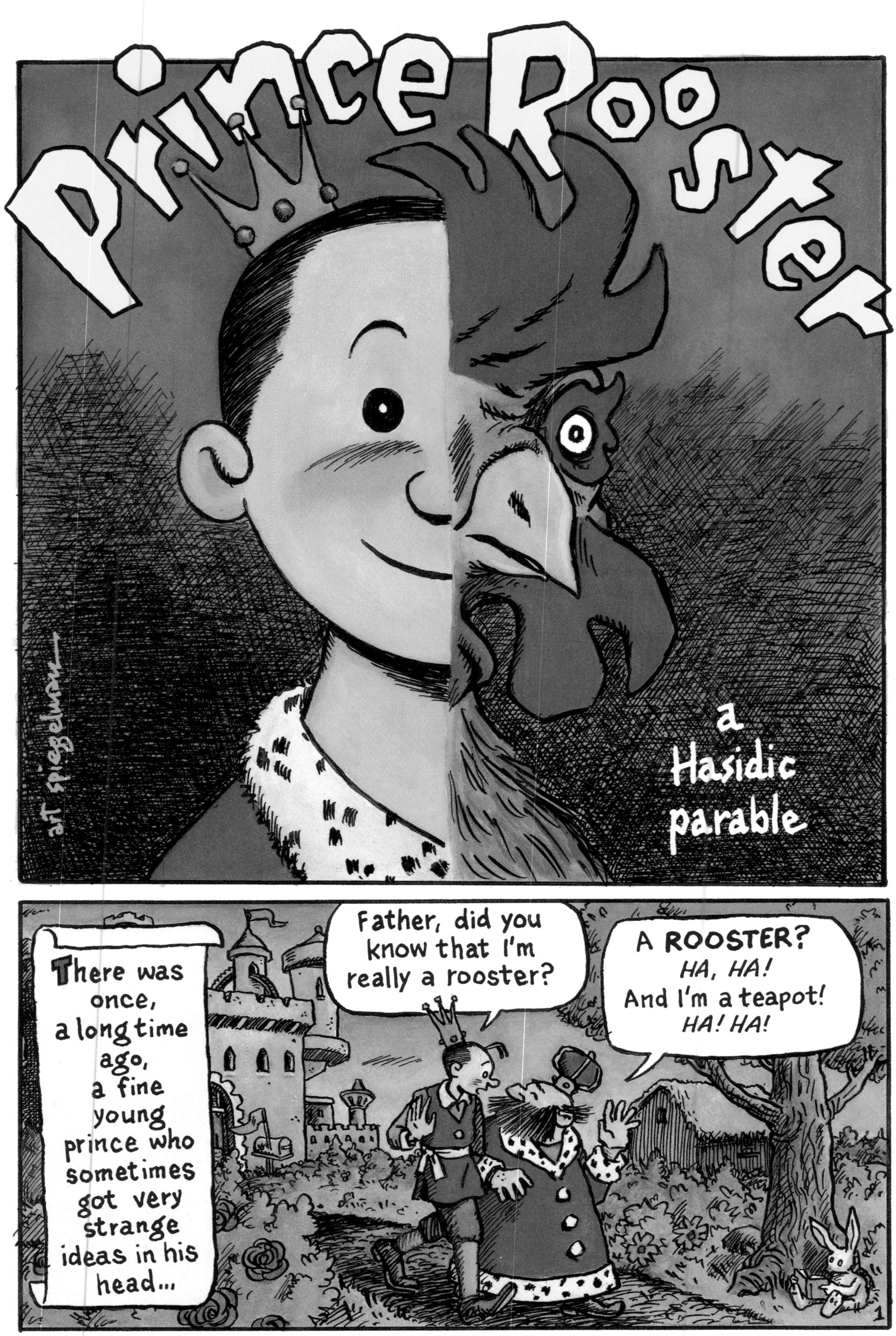
Prince Rooster
art spiegelman
a Hasidic parable
There was once, a long time ago, a fine young prince who sometimes got very strange ideas in his head...
Father, did you know that I'm really a rooster?
A **ROOSTER?** *HA, HA!* And I'm a teapot! *HA! HA!*
1

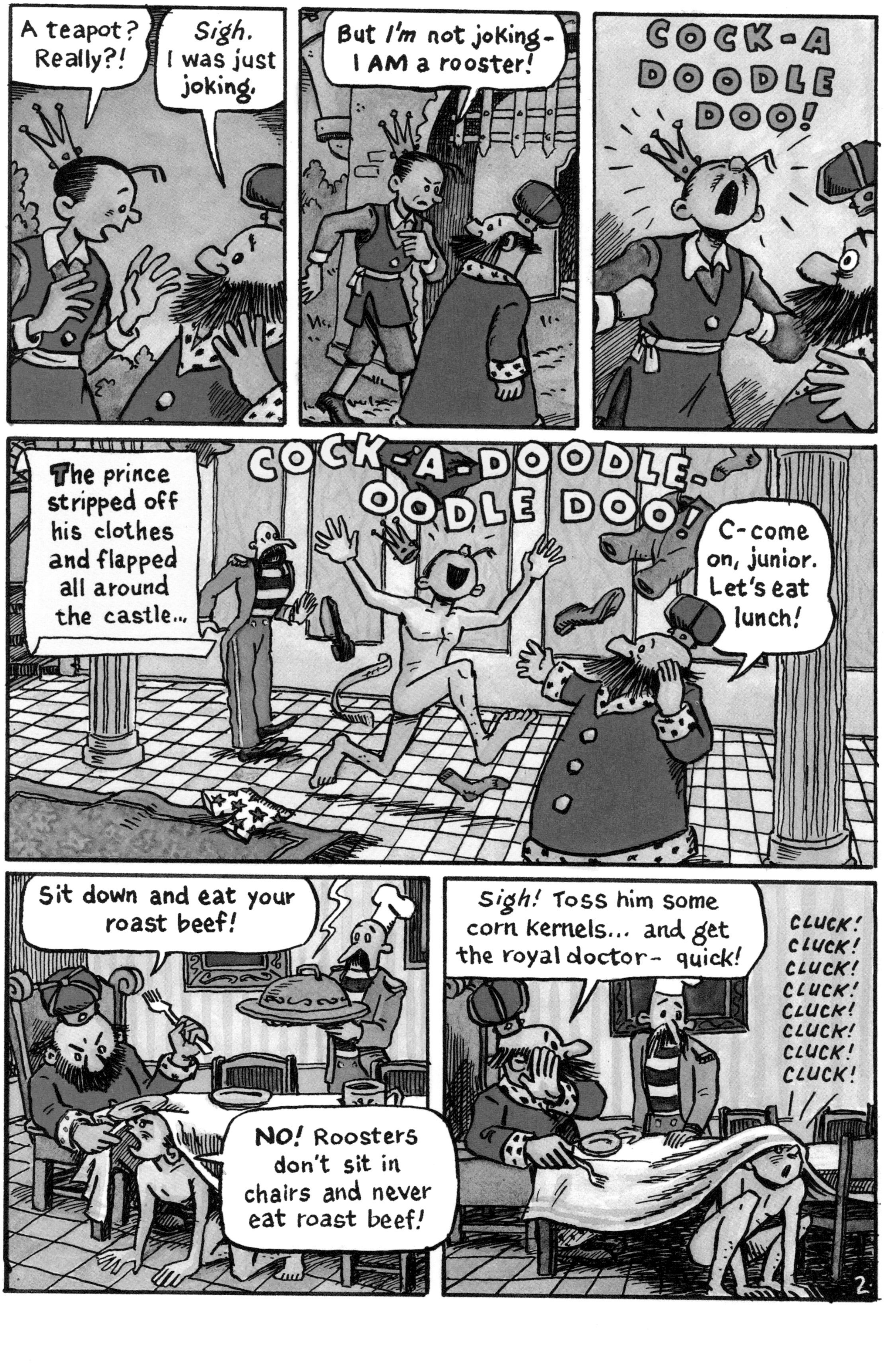
A teapot? Really?!
Sigh. I was just joking.
But I'm not joking- I AM a rooster!
COCK-A DOODLE DOO!
The prince stripped off his clothes and flapped all around the castle...
COCK-A-DOODLE-OODLE DOO!
C-come on, junior. Let's eat lunch!
Sit down and eat your roast beef!
NO! Roosters don't sit in chairs and never eat roast beef!
Sigh! Toss him some corn kernels... and get the royal doctor- quick!
CLUCK! CLUCK! CLUCK! CLUCK! CLUCK! CLUCK! CLUCK! CLUCK!
2

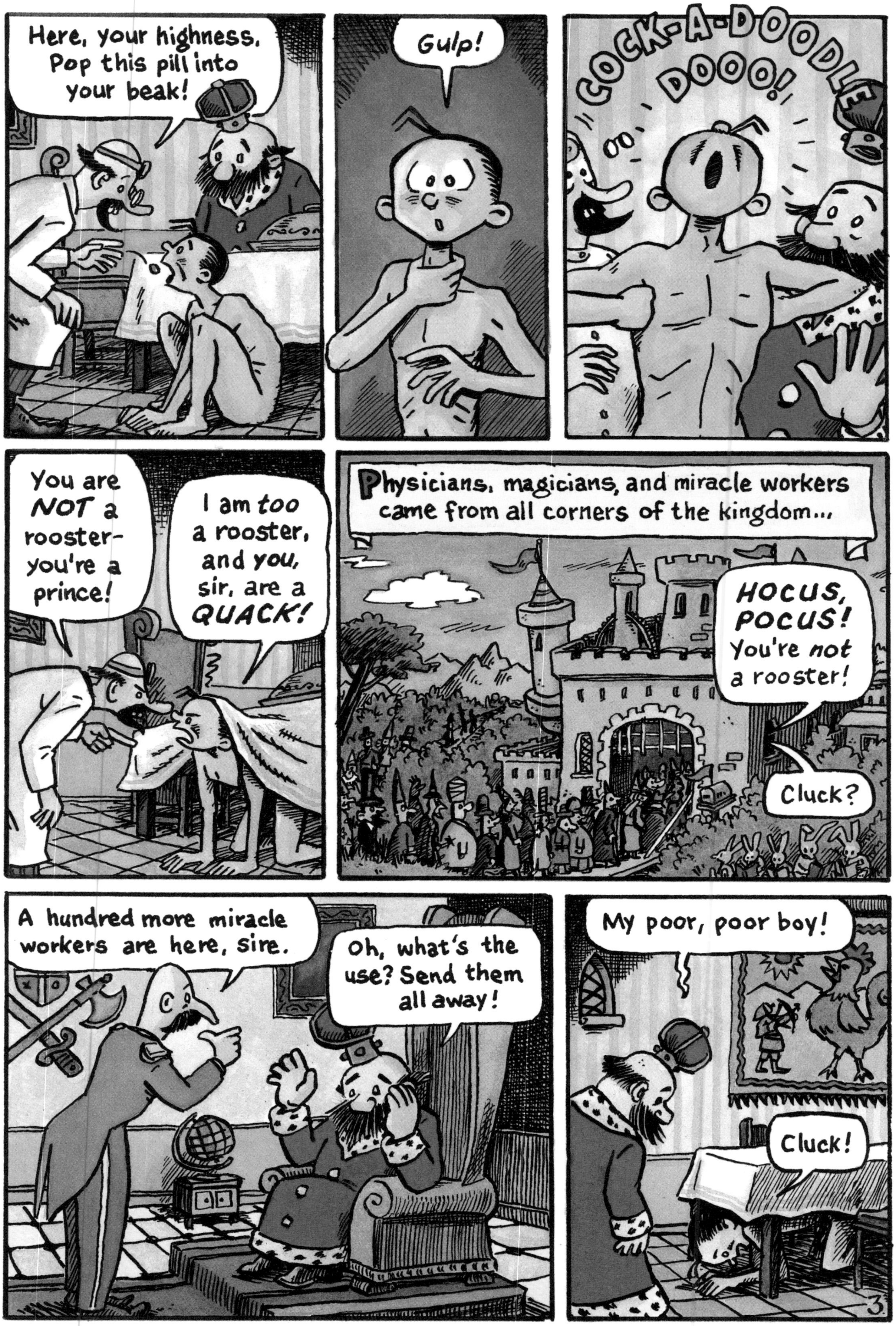
Here, your highness. Pop this pill into your beak!
Gulp!
COCK-A-DOODLE DOOO!
You are NOT a rooster- you're a prince!
I am too a rooster, and you, sir, are a QUACK!
Physicians, magicians, and miracle workers came from all corners of the kingdom...
HOCUS, POCUS! You're not a rooster!
Cluck?
A hundred more miracle workers are here, sire.
Oh, what's the use? Send them all away!
My poor, poor boy!
Cluck!
3

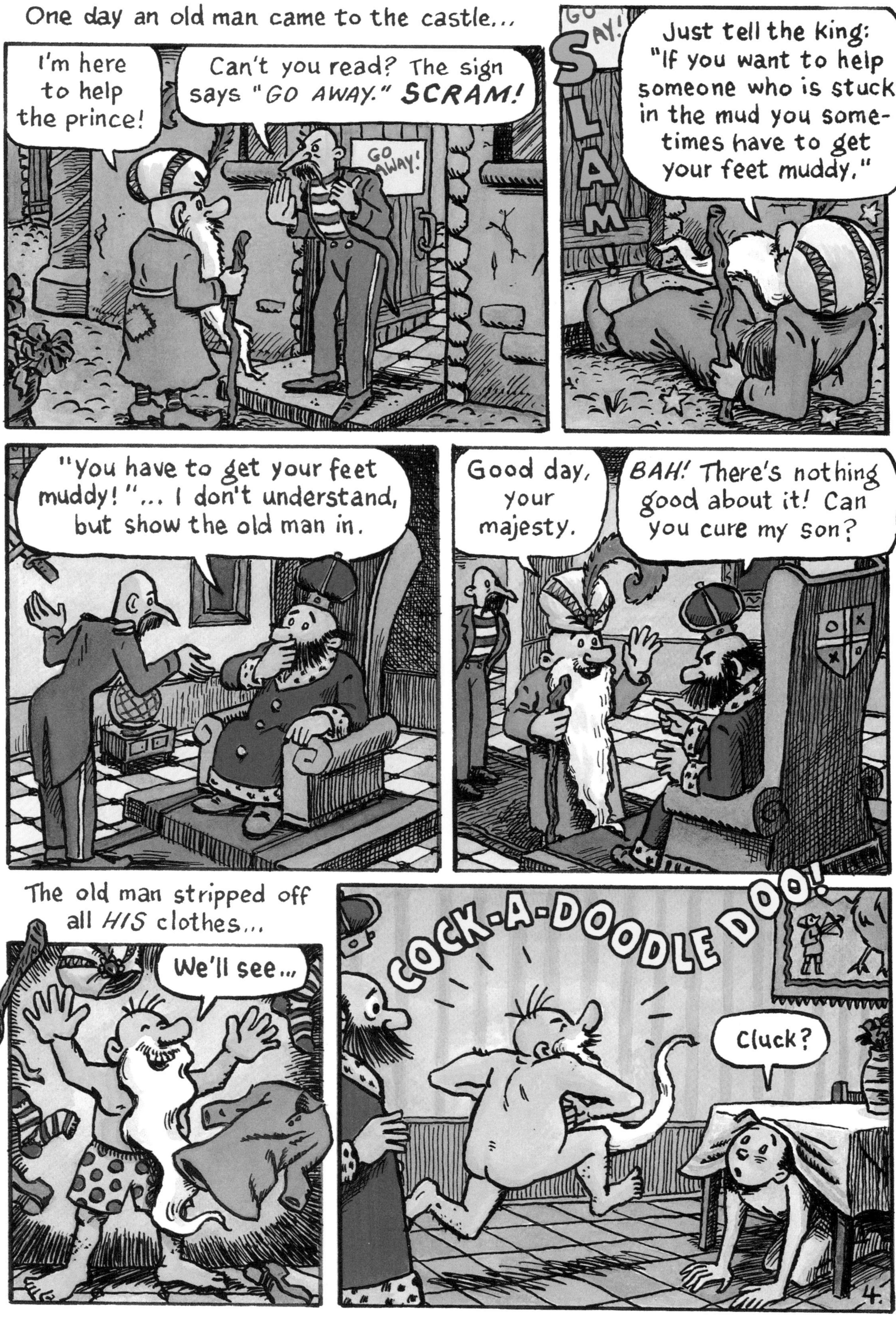
One day an old man came to the castle...
I'm here to help the prince!
Can't you read? The sign says "GO AWAY." SCRAM!
GO AWAY!
SLAM!
Just tell the king: "If you want to help someone who is stuck in the mud you sometimes have to get your feet muddy."
"You have to get your feet muddy!"... I don't understand, but show the old man in.
Good day, your majesty.
BAH! There's nothing good about it! Can you cure my son?
The old man stripped off all HIS clothes...
We'll see...
COCK-A-DOODLE DOO!
Cluck?
4.

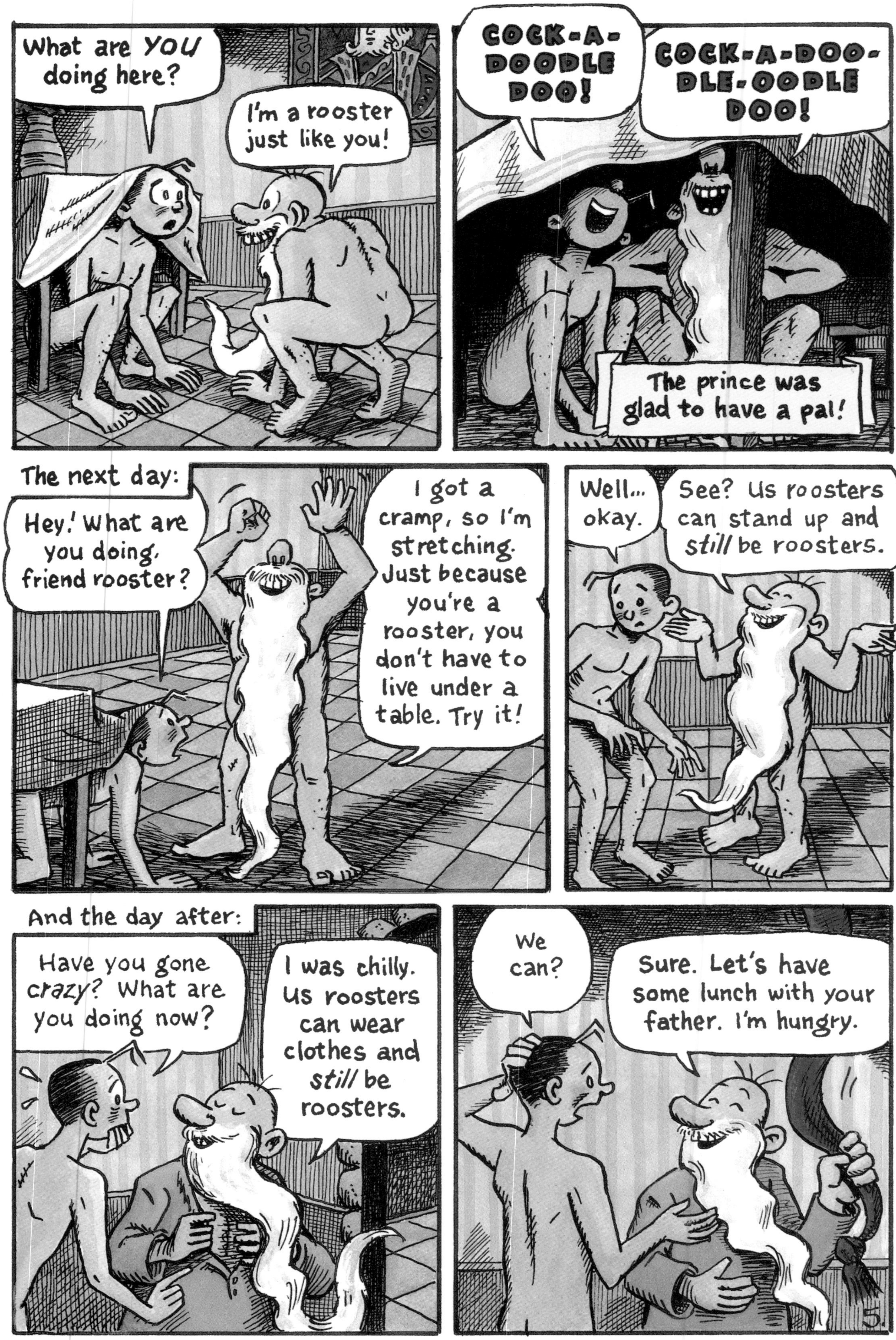
What are YOU doing here?
I'm a rooster just like you!
COCK-A-DOODLE DOO!
COCK-A-DOO-DLE-OODLE DOO!
The prince was glad to have a pal!
The next day:
Hey! What are you doing, friend rooster?
I got a cramp, so I'm stretching. Just because you're a rooster, you don't have to live under a table. Try it!
Well... okay.
See? Us roosters can stand up and *still* be roosters.
And the day after:
Have you gone *crazy*? What are you doing now?
I was chilly. Us roosters can wear clothes and *still* be roosters.
We can?
Sure. Let's have some lunch with your father. I'm hungry.
5.

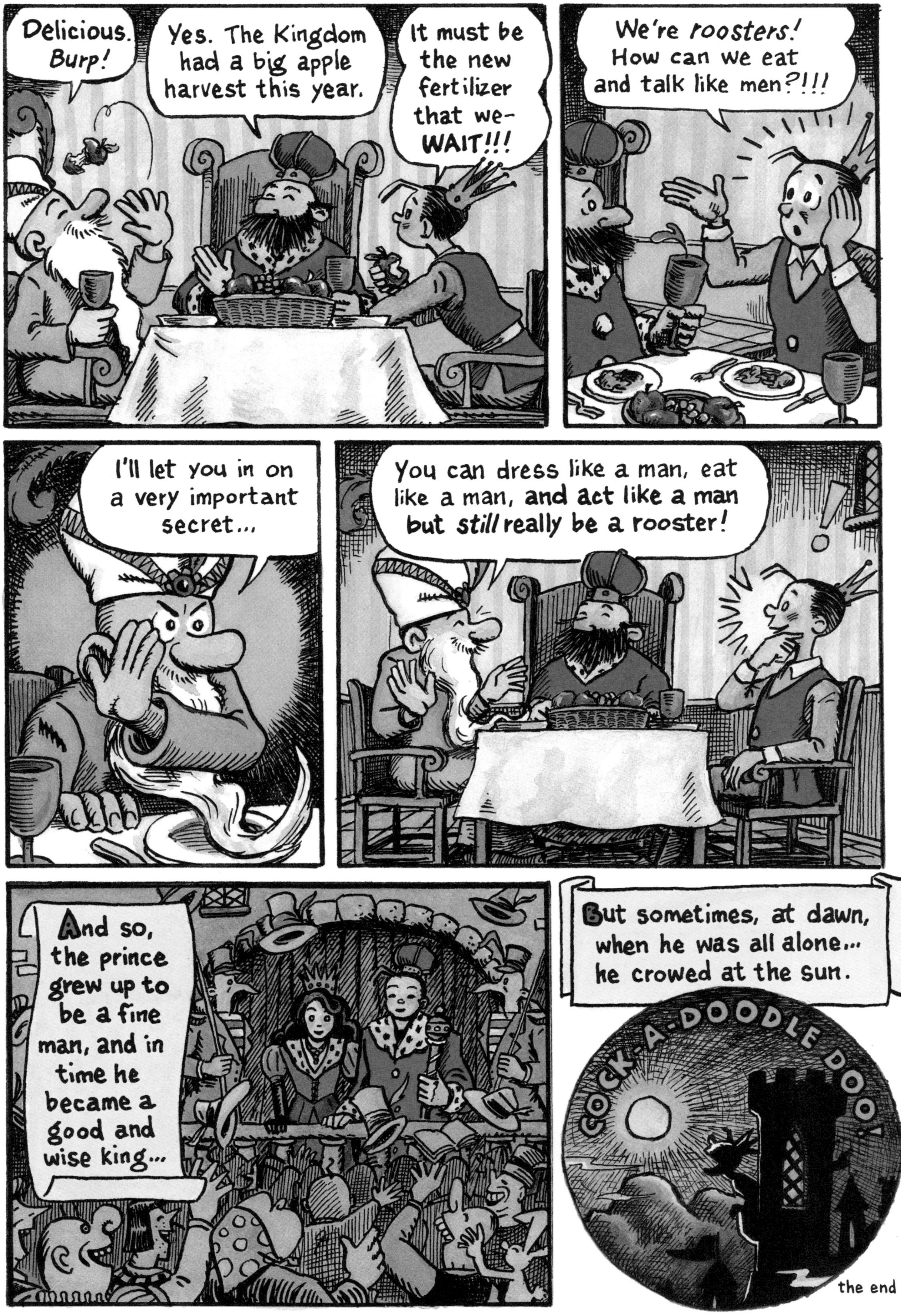
Delicious. *Burp!*
Yes. The Kingdom had a big apple harvest this year.
It must be the new fertilizer that we- WAIT!!!
We're *roosters!* How can we eat and talk like men?!!!
I'll let you in on a very important secret...
You can dress like a man, eat like a man, and act like a man but *still* really be a rooster!
!
And so, the prince grew up to be a fine man, and in time he became a good and wise king...
But sometimes, at dawn, when he was all alone... he crowed at the sun.
COCK-A-DOODLE-DOO!
the end

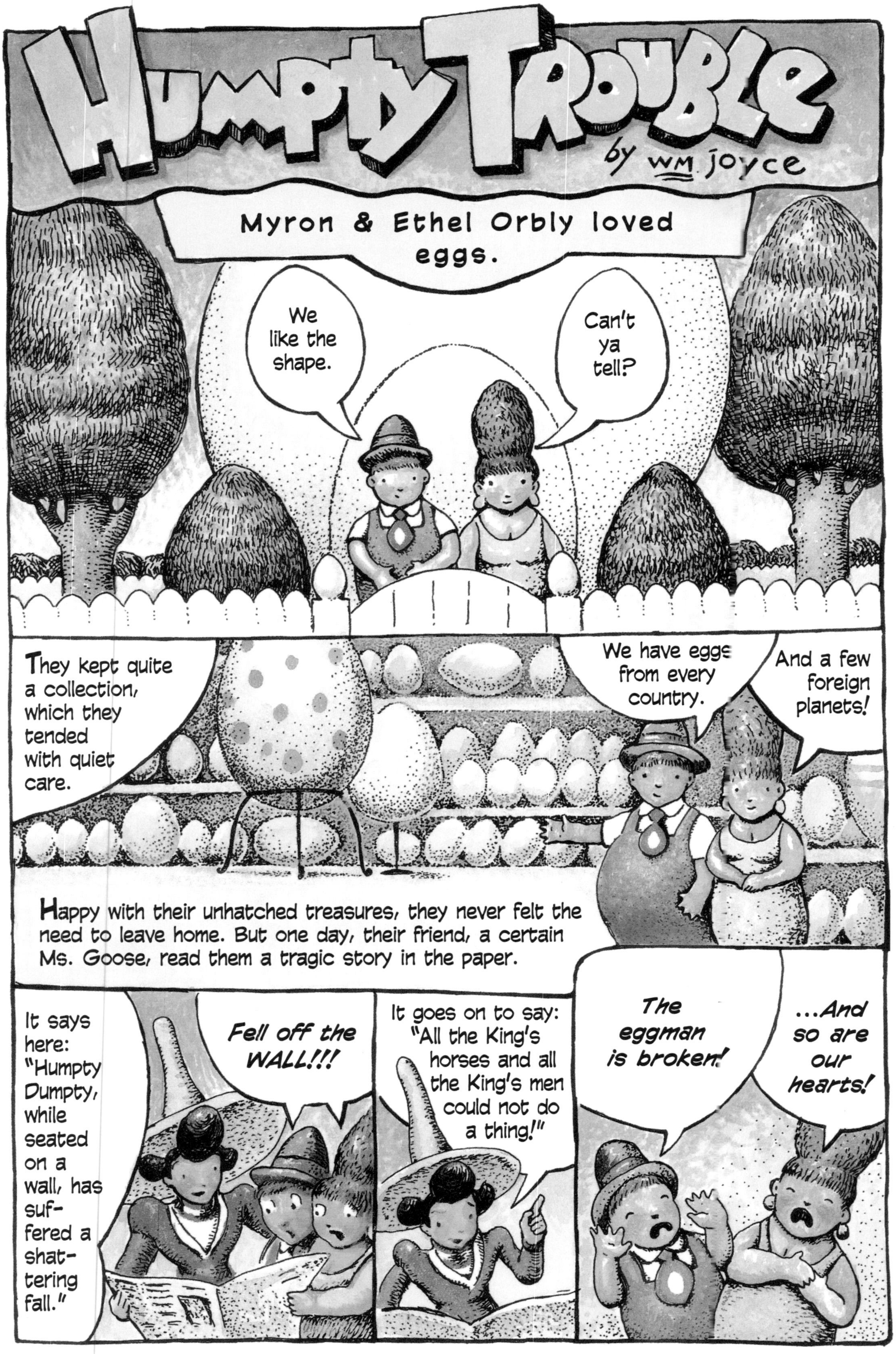
HUMPTY TROUBLE
by Wm Joyce
Myron & Ethel Orbly loved eggs.
We like the shape.
Can't ya tell?
They kept quite a collection, which they tended with quiet care.
We have eggs from every country.
And a few foreign planets!
Happy with their unhatched treasures, they never felt the need to leave home. But one day, their friend, a certain Ms. Goose, read them a tragic story in the paper.
It says here: "Humpty Dumpty, while seated on a wall, has suffered a shattering fall."
Fell off the WALL!!!
It goes on to say: "All the King's horses and all the King's men could not do a thing!"
The eggman is broken!
...And so are our hearts!

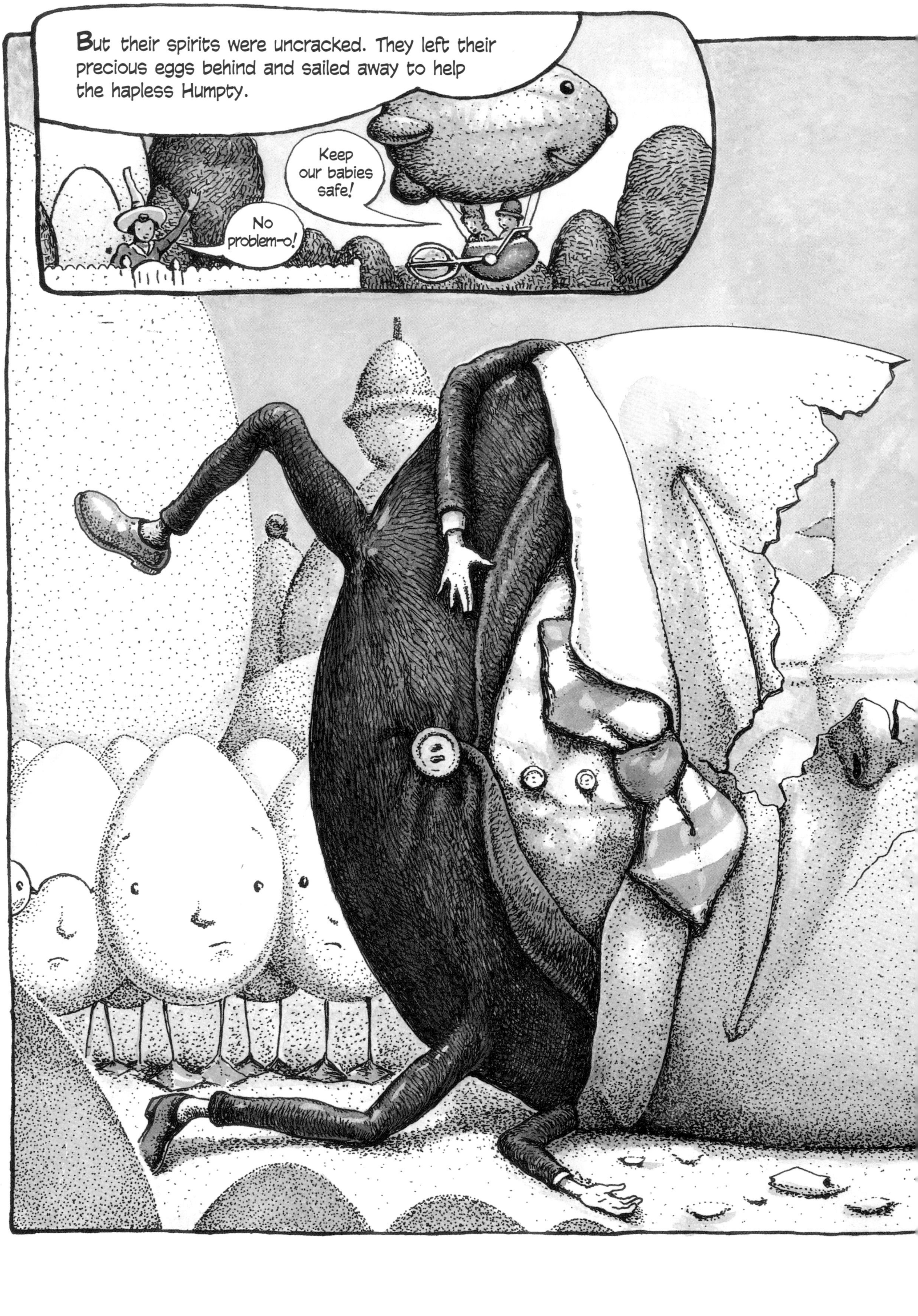
But their spirits were uncracked. They left their precious eggs behind and sailed away to help the hapless Humpty.
Keep our babies safe!
No problem-o!

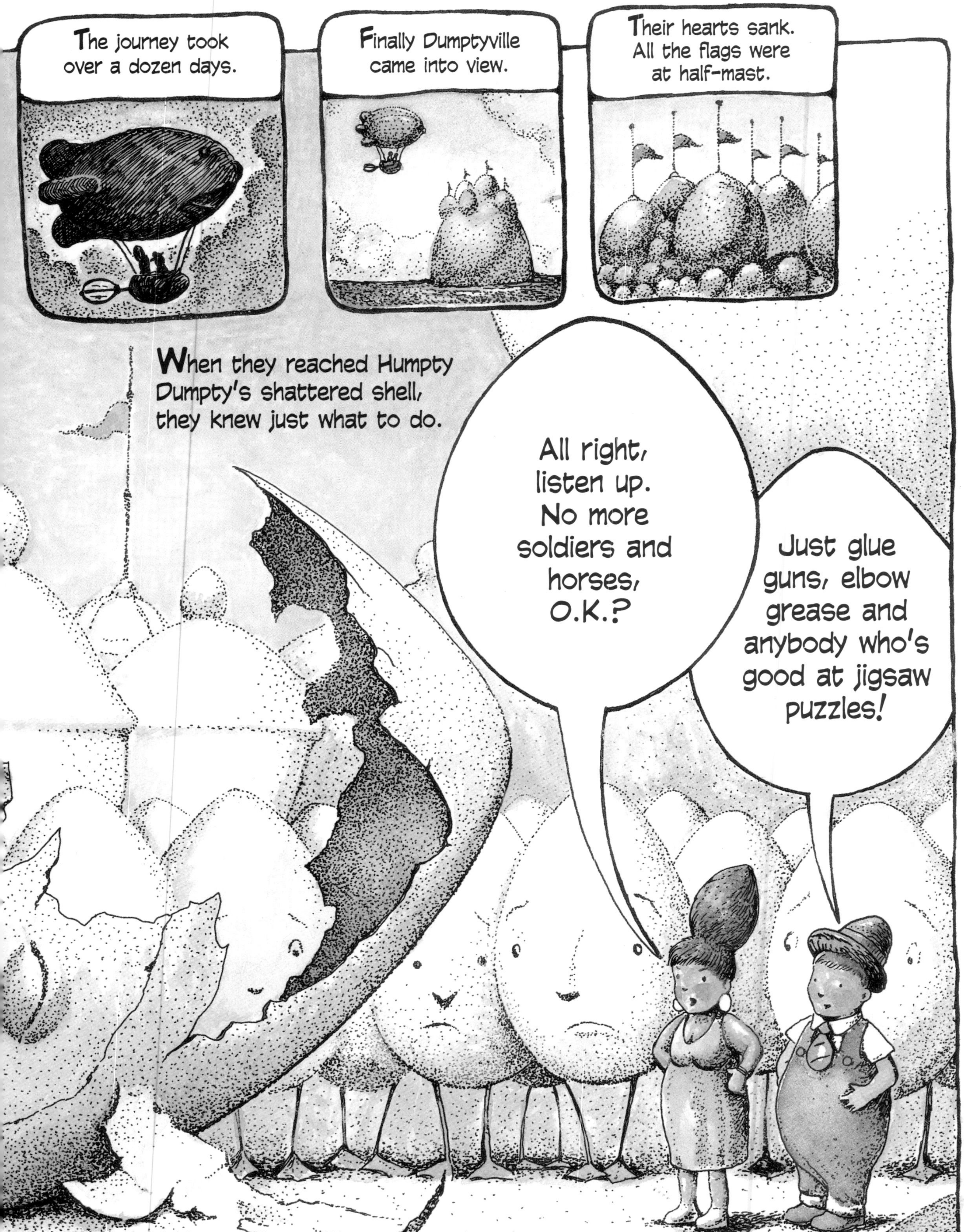
The journey took over a dozen days.
Finally Dumptyville came into view.
Their hearts sank. All the flags were at half-mast.
When they reached Humpty Dumpty's shattered shell, they knew just what to do.
All right, listen up. No more soldiers and horses, O.K.?
Just glue guns, elbow grease and anybody who's good at jigsaw puzzles!

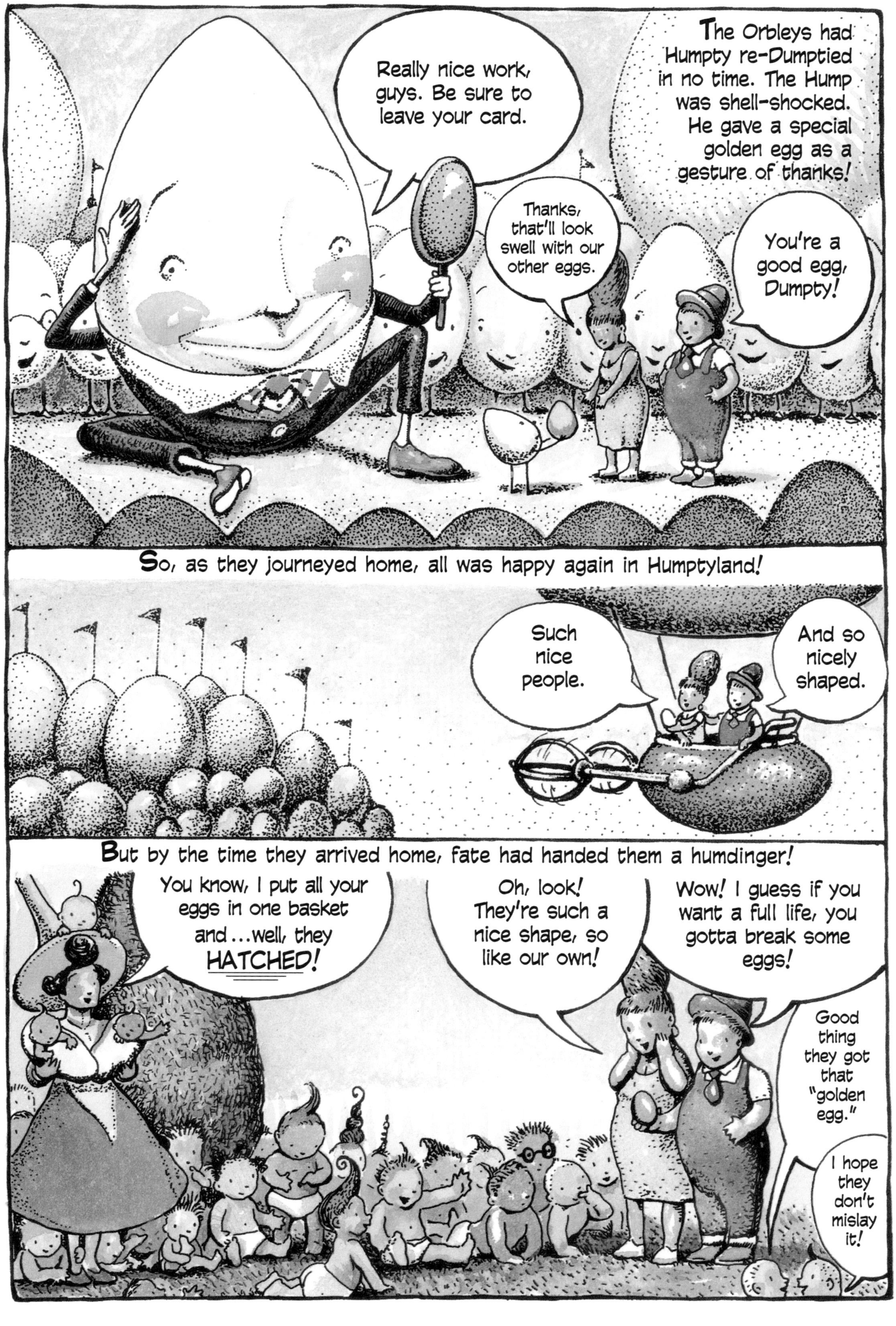
Really nice work, guys. Be sure to leave your card.
The Orbleys had Humpty re-Dumptied in no time. The Hump was shell-shocked. He gave a special golden egg as a gesture of thanks!
Thanks, that'll look swell with our other eggs.
You're a good egg, Dumpty!
So, as they journeyed home, all was happy again in Humptyland!
Such nice people.
And so nicely shaped.
But by the time they arrived home, fate had handed them a humdinger!
You know, I put all your eggs in one basket and...well, they HATCHED!
Oh, look! They're such a nice shape, so like our own!
Wow! I guess if you want a full life, you gotta break some eggs!
Good thing they got that "golden egg."
I hope they don't mislay it!

A KNIGHT TO REMEMBER

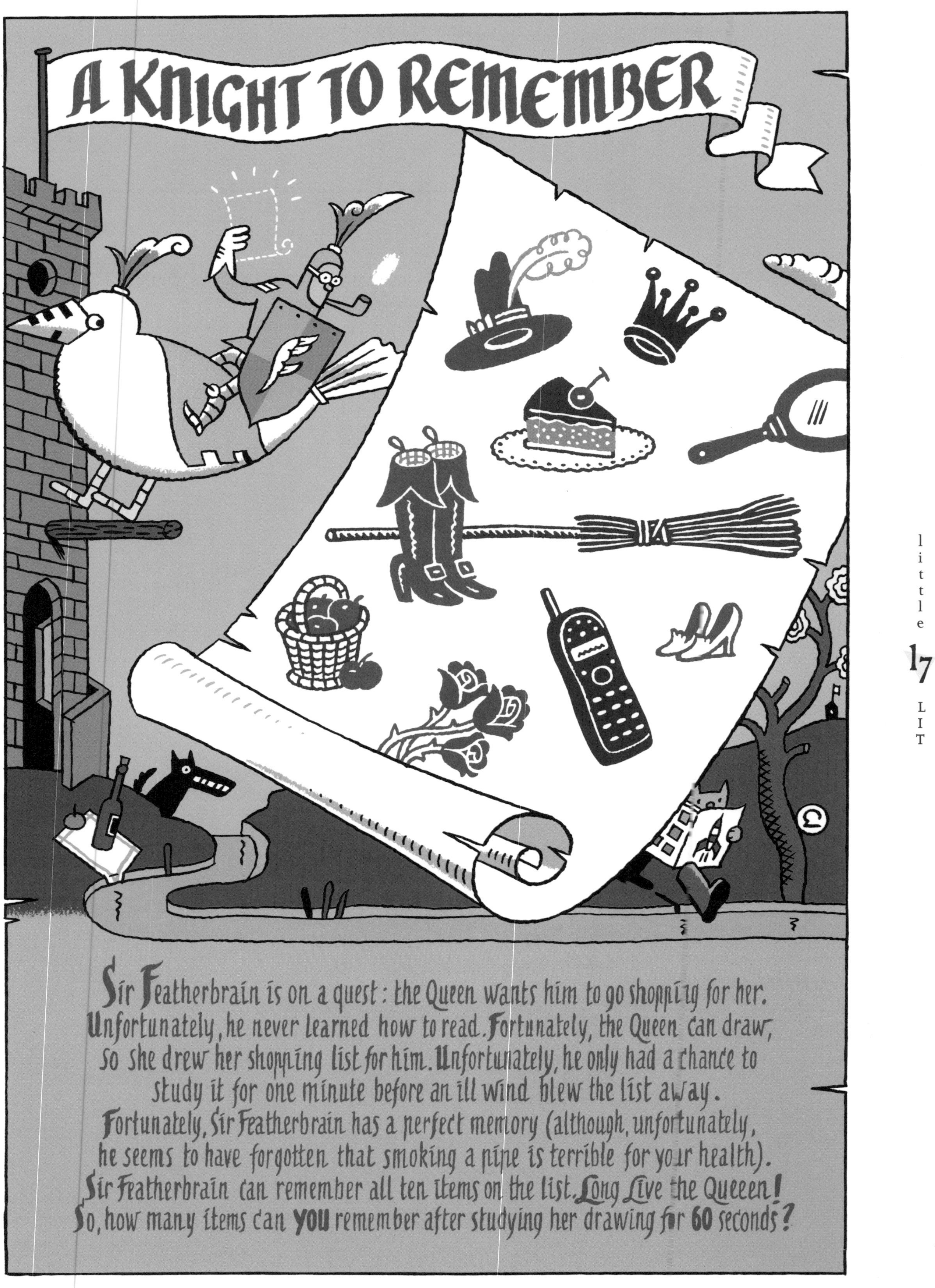

Sir Featherbrain is on a quest: the Queen wants him to go shopping for her. Unfortunately, he never learned how to read. Fortunately, the Queen can draw, so she drew her shopping list for him. Unfortunately, he only had a chance to study it for one minute before an ill wind blew the list away. Fortunately, Sir Featherbrain has a perfect memory (although, unfortunately, he seems to have forgotten that smoking a pipe is terrible for your health). Sir Featherbrain can remember all ten items on the list. Long Live the Queeen! So, how many items can **YOU** remember after studying her drawing for **60** seconds?

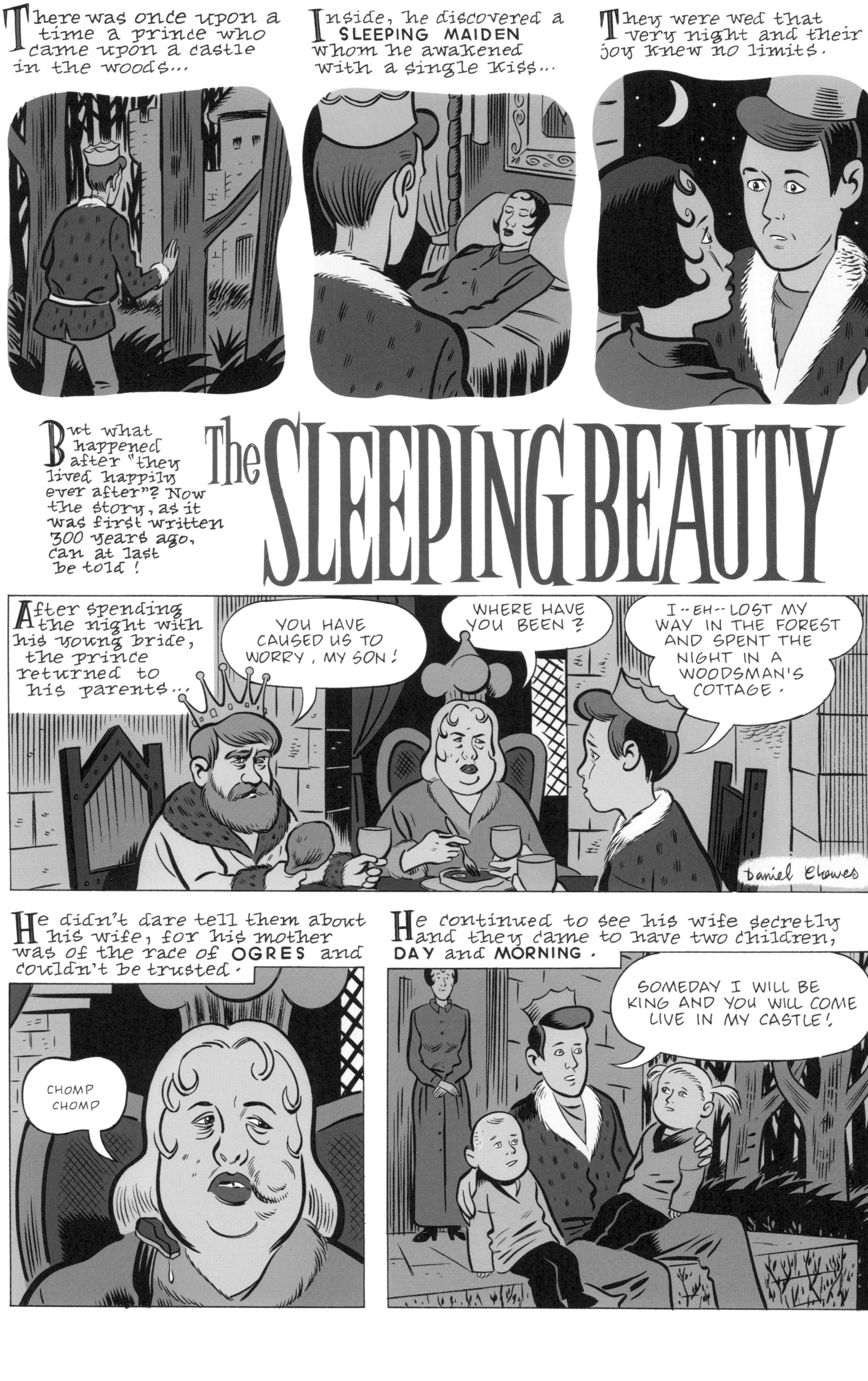
There was once upon a time a prince who came upon a castle in the woods...
Inside, he discovered a SLEEPING MAIDEN whom he awakened with a single kiss...
They were wed that very night and their joy knew no limits.
But what happened after "they lived happily ever after"? Now the story, as it was first written 300 years ago, can at last be told!
The SLEEPING BEAUTY
After spending the night with his young bride, the prince returned to his parents...
YOU HAVE CAUSED US TO WORRY, MY SON!
WHERE HAVE YOU BEEN?
I--EH--LOST MY WAY IN THE FOREST AND SPENT THE NIGHT IN A WOODSMAN'S COTTAGE.
Daniel Clowes
He didn't dare tell them about his wife, for his mother was of the race of OGRES and couldn't be trusted.
CHOMP CHOMP
He continued to see his wife secretly and they came to have two children, DAY and MORNING.
SOMEDAY I WILL BE KING AND YOU WILL COME LIVE IN MY CASTLE!

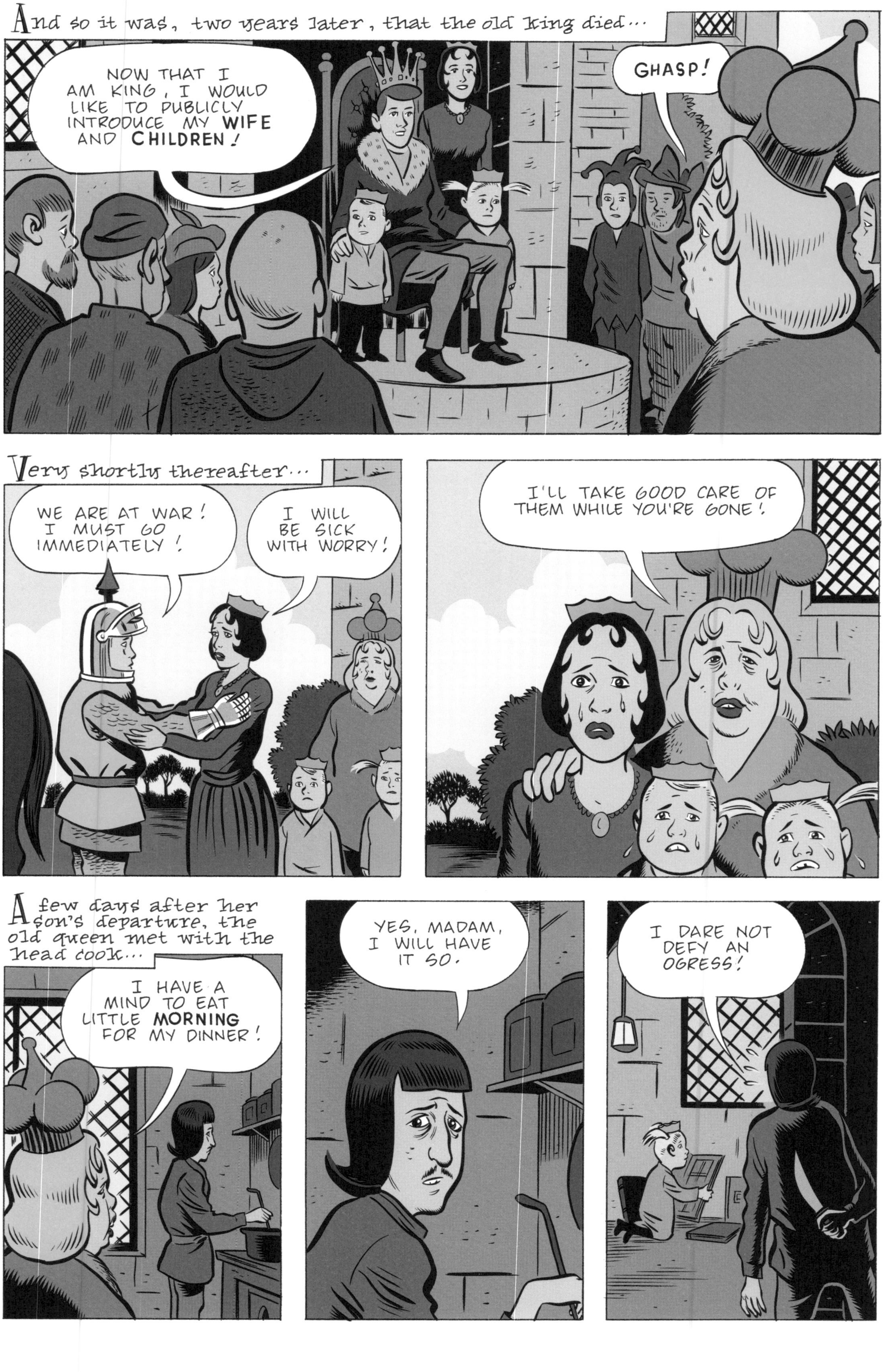
And so it was, two years later, that the old King died...
NOW THAT I AM KING, I WOULD LIKE TO PUBLICLY INTRODUCE MY WIFE AND CHILDREN!
GHASP!
Very shortly thereafter...
WE ARE AT WAR! I MUST GO IMMEDIATELY!
I WILL BE SICK WITH WORRY!
I'LL TAKE GOOD CARE OF THEM WHILE YOU'RE GONE!
A few days after her son's departure, the old queen met with the head cook...
I HAVE A MIND TO EAT LITTLE MORNING FOR MY DINNER!
YES, MADAM, I WILL HAVE IT SO.
I DARE NOT DEFY AN OGRESS!

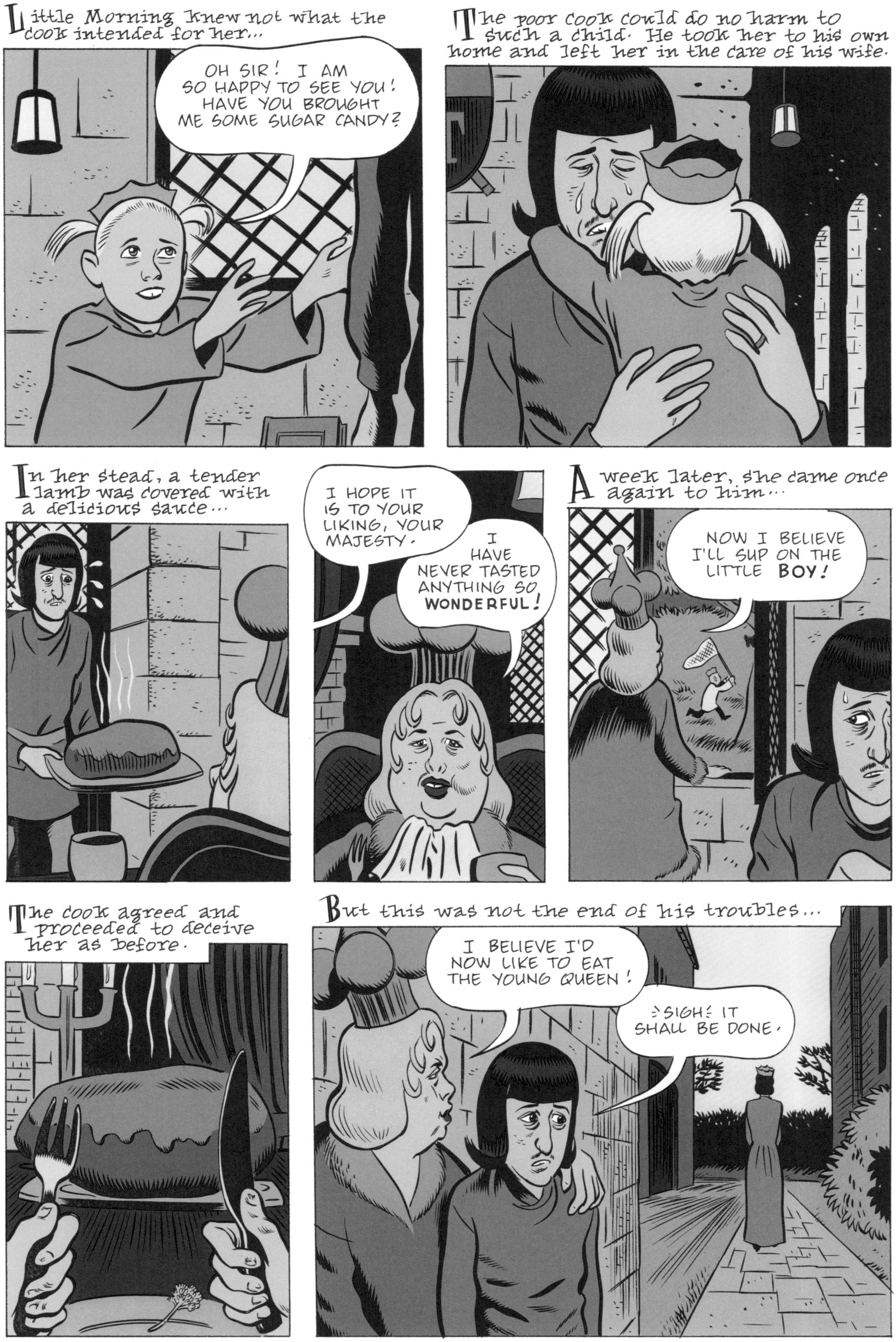
Little Morning knew not what the cook intended for her...
OH SIR! I AM SO HAPPY TO SEE YOU! HAVE YOU BROUGHT ME SOME SUGAR CANDY?
The poor cook could do no harm to such a child. He took her to his own home and left her in the care of his wife.
In her stead, a tender lamb was covered with a delicious sauce...
I HOPE IT IS TO YOUR LIKING, YOUR MAJESTY.
I HAVE NEVER TASTED ANYTHING SO WONDERFUL!
A week later, she came once again to him...
NOW I BELIEVE I'LL SUP ON THE LITTLE BOY!
The cook agreed and proceeded to deceive her as before.
But this was not the end of his troubles...
I BELIEVE I'D NOW LIKE TO EAT THE YOUNG QUEEN!
SIGH IT SHALL BE DONE.

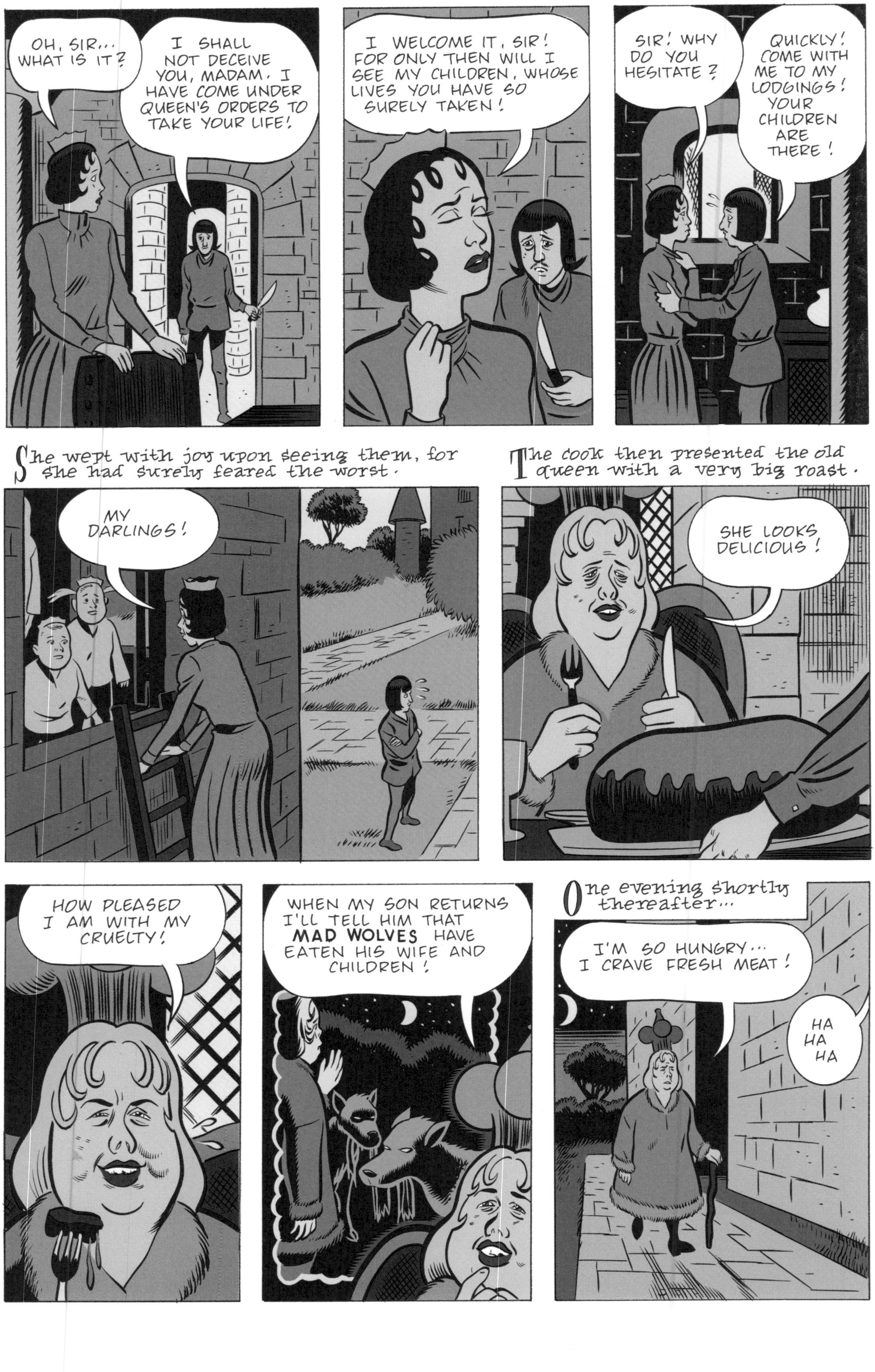
OH, SIR... WHAT IS IT?
I SHALL NOT DECEIVE YOU, MADAM. I HAVE COME UNDER QUEEN'S ORDERS TO TAKE YOUR LIFE!
I WELCOME IT, SIR! FOR ONLY THEN WILL I SEE MY CHILDREN, WHOSE LIVES YOU HAVE SO SURELY TAKEN!
SIR! WHY DO YOU HESITATE?
QUICKLY! COME WITH ME TO MY LODGINGS! YOUR CHILDREN ARE THERE!
She wept with joy upon seeing them, for she had surely feared the worst.
MY DARLINGS!
The cook then presented the old queen with a very big roast.
SHE LOOKS DELICIOUS!
HOW PLEASED I AM WITH MY CRUELTY!
WHEN MY SON RETURNS I'LL TELL HIM THAT MAD WOLVES HAVE EATEN HIS WIFE AND CHILDREN!
One evening shortly thereafter...
I'M SO HUNGRY... I CRAVE FRESH MEAT!
HA HA HA

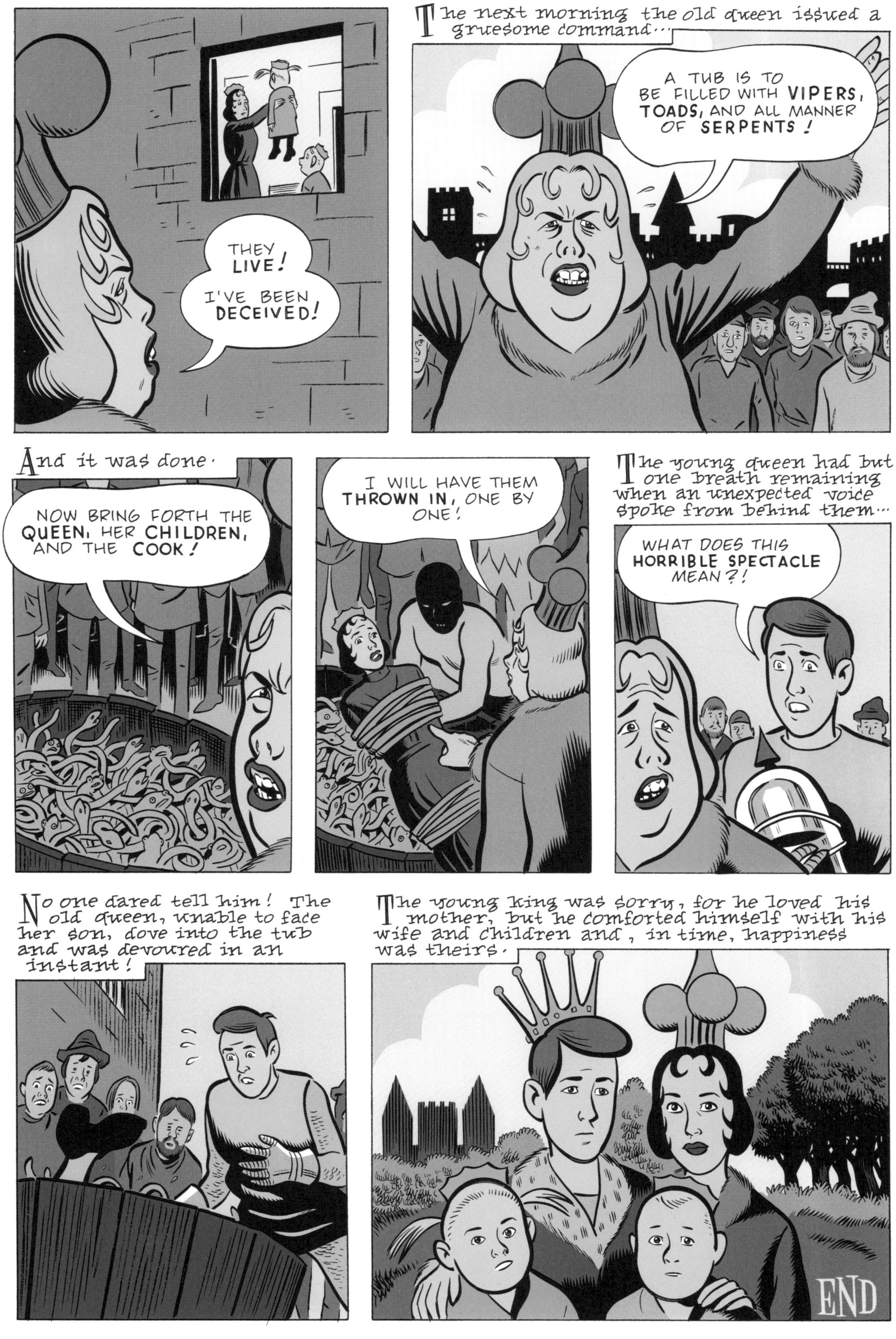
THEY LIVE! I'VE BEEN DECEIVED!
The next morning the old queen issued a gruesome command...
A TUB IS TO BE FILLED WITH VIPERS, TOADS, AND ALL MANNER OF SERPENTS!
And it was done.
NOW BRING FORTH THE QUEEN, HER CHILDREN, AND THE COOK!
I WILL HAVE THEM THROWN IN, ONE BY ONE!
The young queen had but one breath remaining when an unexpected voice spoke from behind them...
WHAT DOES THIS HORRIBLE SPECTACLE MEAN?!
No one dared tell him! The old queen, unable to face her son, dove into the tub and was devoured in an instant!
The young king was sorry, for he loved his mother, but he comforted himself with his wife and children and, in time, happiness was theirs.
END

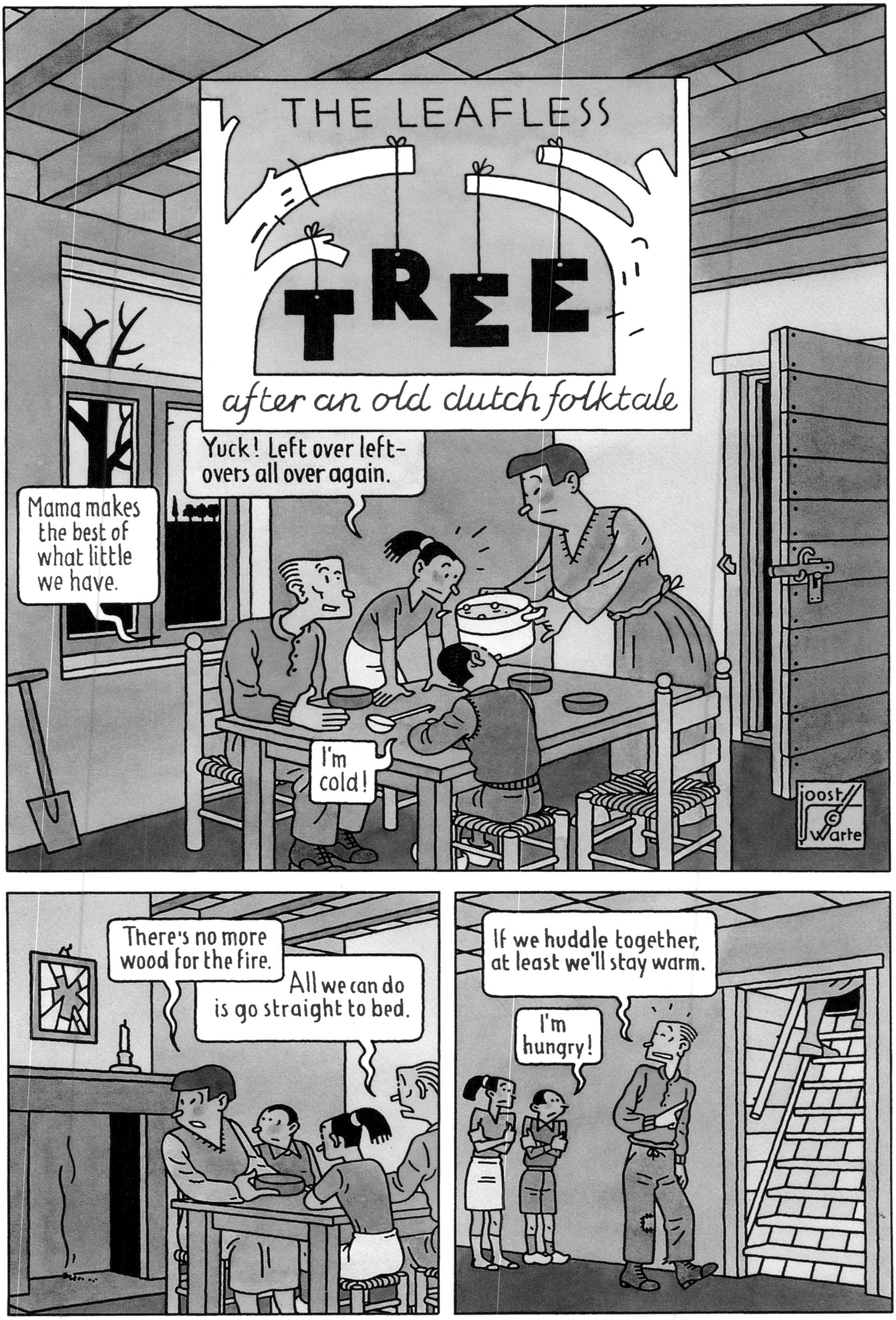
THE LEAFLESS
TREE
after an old dutch folktale
Mama makes the best of what little we have.
Yuck! Left over left-overs all over again.
I'm cold!
joost Swarte
There's no more wood for the fire.
All we can do is go straight to bed.
If we huddle together, at least we'll stay warm.
I'm hungry!

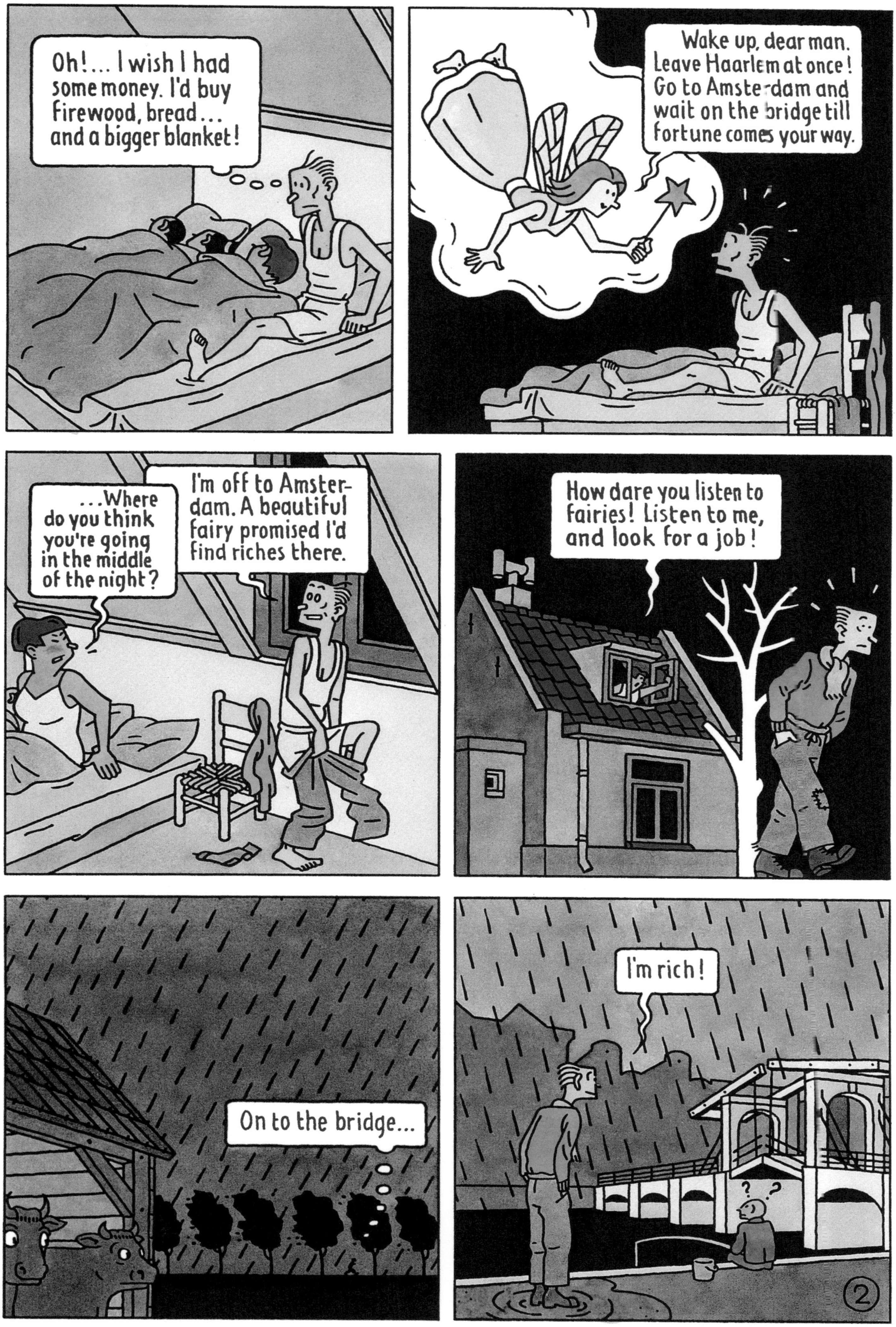
Oh!... I wish I had some money. I'd buy firewood, bread... and a bigger blanket!
Wake up, dear man. Leave Haarlem at once! Go to Amsterdam and wait on the bridge till fortune comes your way.
...Where do you think you're going in the middle of the night?
I'm off to Amsterdam. A beautiful fairy promised I'd find riches there.
How dare you listen to fairies! Listen to me, and look for a job!
On to the bridge...
I'm rich!
? ?
2

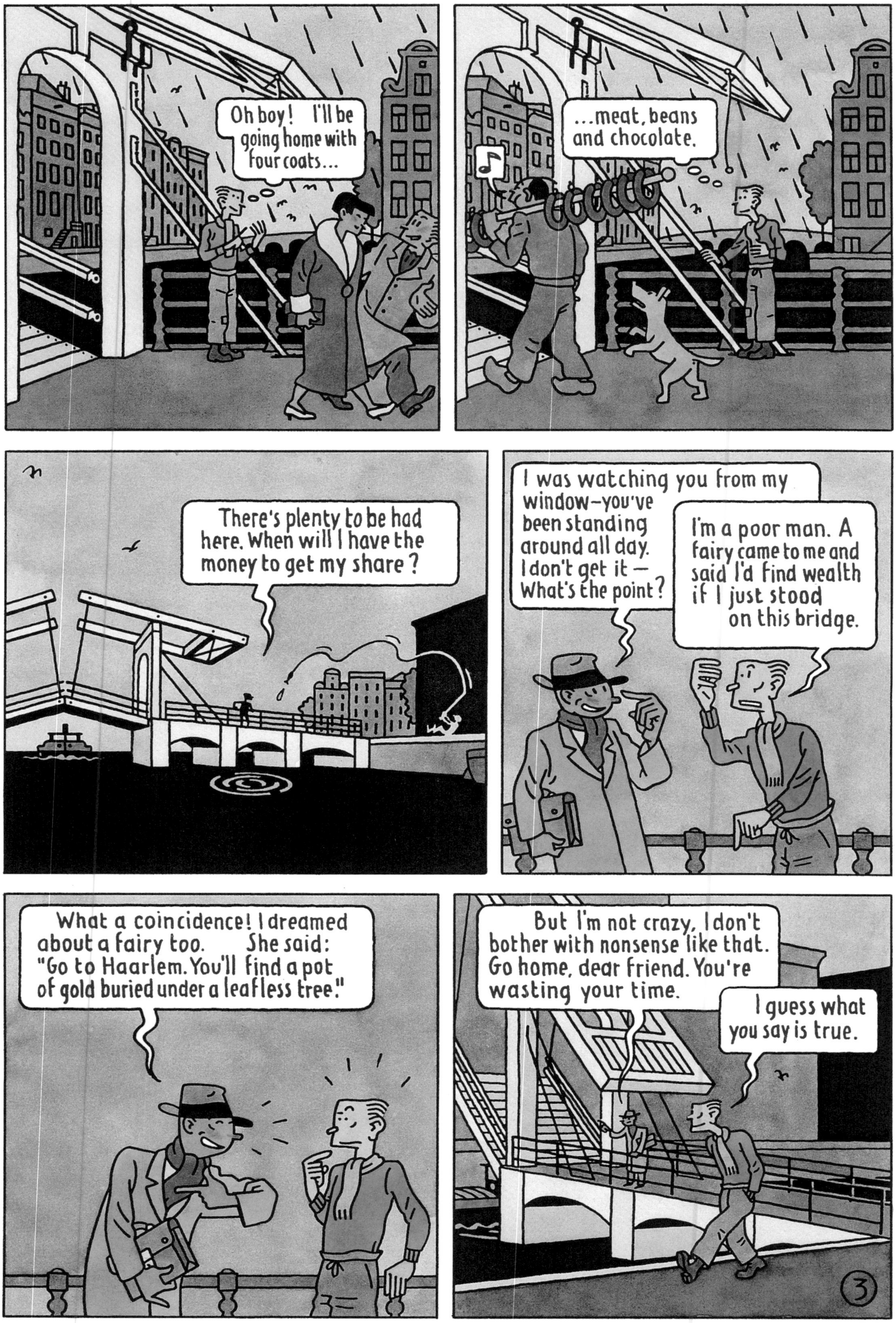
Oh boy! I'll be going home with four coats...
...meat, beans and chocolate.
There's plenty to be had here. When will I have the money to get my share?
I was watching you from my window—you've been standing around all day. I don't get it— What's the point?
I'm a poor man. A fairy came to me and said I'd find wealth if I just stood on this bridge.
What a coincidence! I dreamed about a fairy too. She said: "Go to Haarlem. You'll find a pot of gold buried under a leafless tree."
But I'm not crazy, I don't bother with nonsense like that. Go home, dear friend. You're wasting your time.
I guess what you say is true.
3

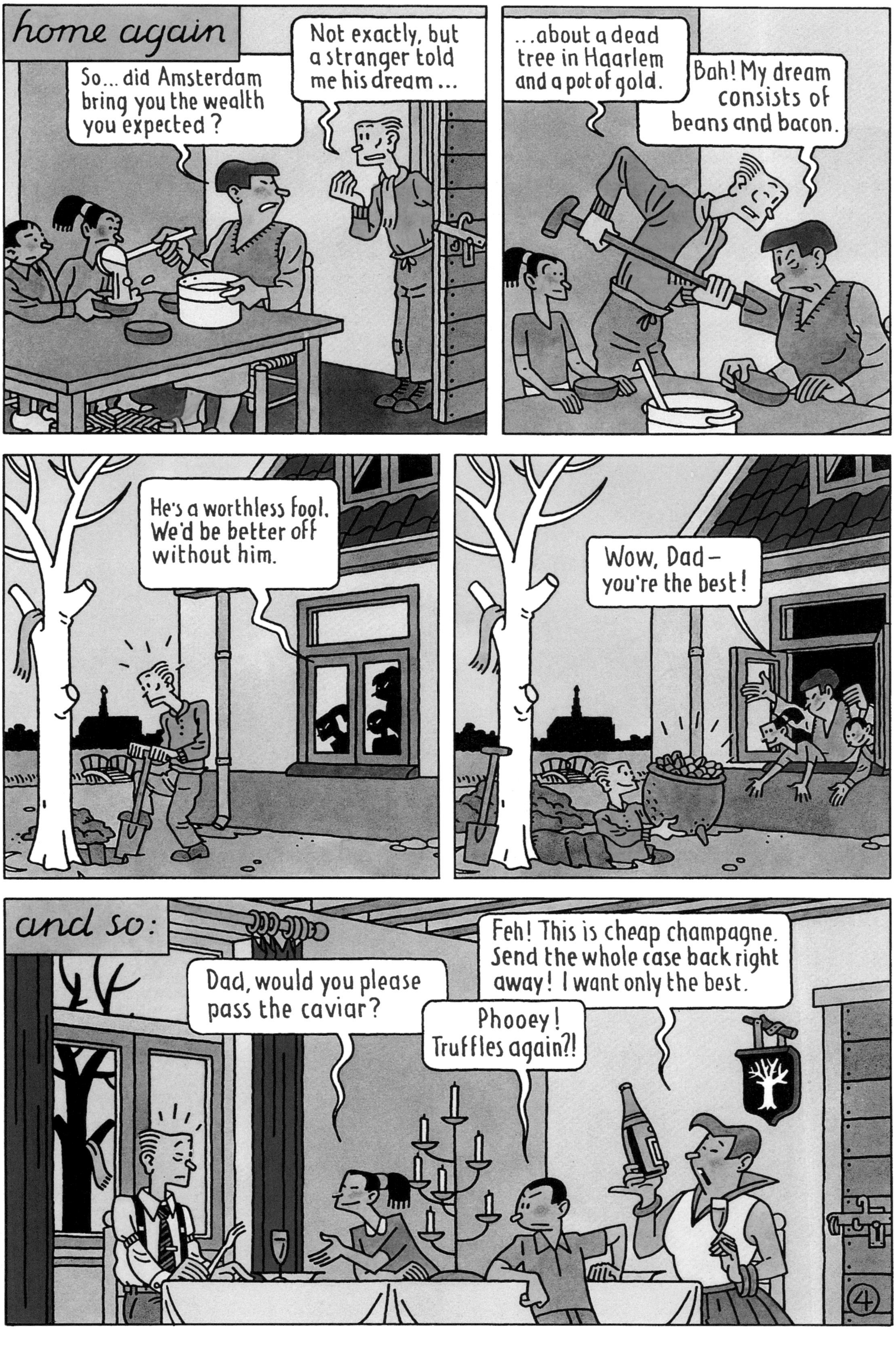
home again
So... did Amsterdam bring you the wealth you expected?
Not exactly, but a stranger told me his dream...
...about a dead tree in Haarlem and a pot of gold.
Bah! My dream consists of beans and bacon.
He's a worthless fool. We'd be better off without him.
Wow, Dad – you're the best!
and so:
Dad, would you please pass the caviar?
Phooey! Truffles again?!
Feh! This is cheap champagne. Send the whole case back right away! I want only the best.

RAPUNZEL'S DARING ESCAPE!

WHAT'S WRONG WITH THIS PICTURE?

Rapunzel, trapped in the Witch's tower, and the Prince, who visits her by climbing her long golden hair, are one of the great couples in fairy tale history. We asked our artist, Bruce McCall, to illustrate the tale, but he is frankly none too bright and has pretty much flubbed it. In fact, his picture is so full of mistakes, we can barely count them all. If you're even twice as smart as we think you are, we bet you'll track down lots of them!

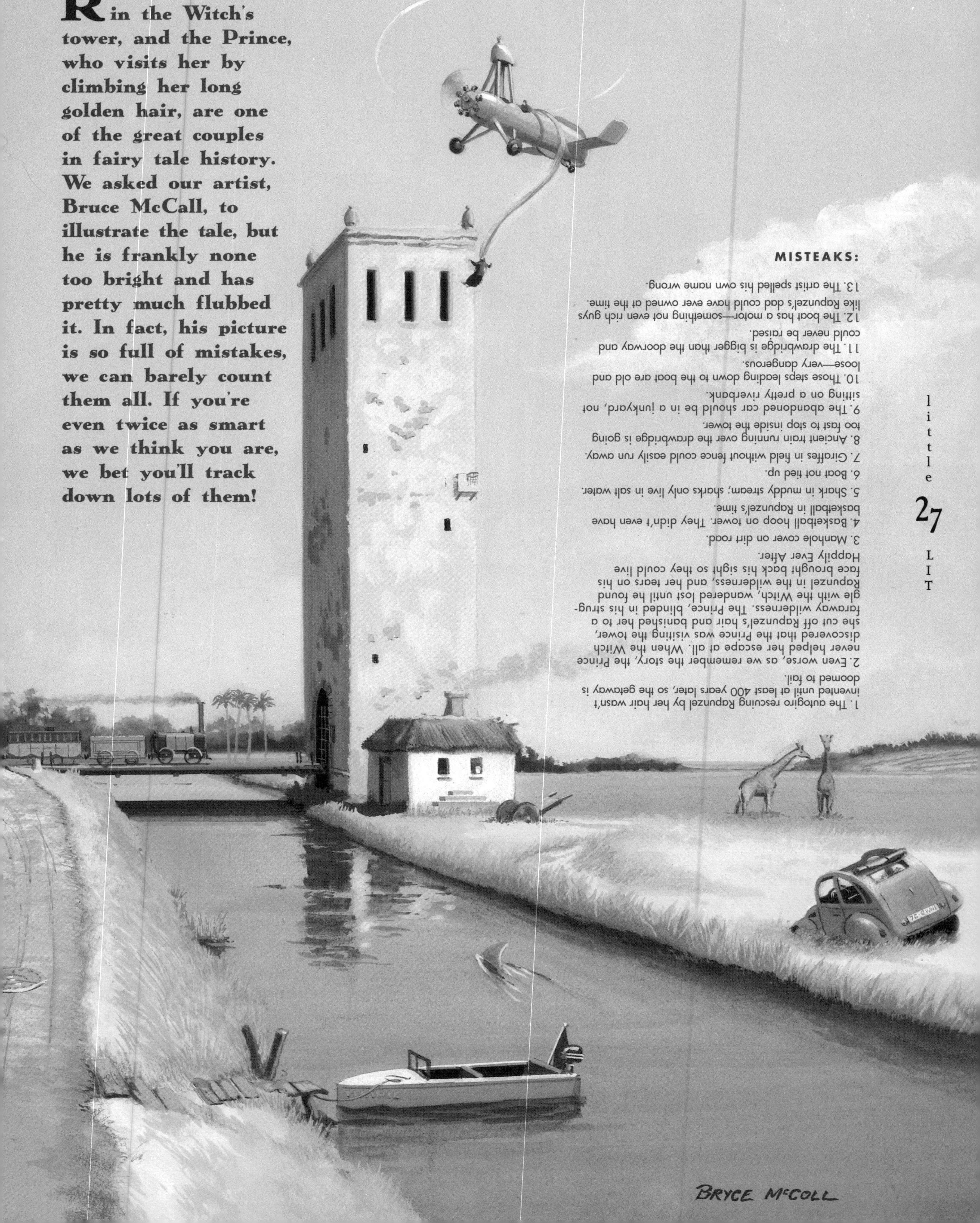
BRYCE McCOLL

MISTEAKS:

1. The autogiro rescuing Rapunzel by her hair wasn't invented until at least 400 years later, so the getaway is doomed to fail.
2. Even worse, as we remember the story, the Prince never helped her escape at all. When the Witch discovered that the Prince was visiting the tower, she cut off Rapunzel's hair and banished her to a faraway wilderness. The Prince, blinded in his struggle with the Witch, wandered lost until he found Rapunzel in the wilderness, and her tears on his face brought back his sight so they could live Happily Ever After.
3. Manhole cover on dirt road.
4. Basketball hoop on tower. They didn't even have basketball in Rapunzel's time.
5. Shark in muddy stream; sharks only live in salt water.
6. Boat not tied up.
7. Giraffes in field without fence could easily run away.
8. Ancient train running over the drawbridge is going too fast to stop inside the tower.
9. The abandoned car should be in a junkyard, not sitting on a pretty riverbank.
10. Those steps leading down to the boat are old and loose—very dangerous.
11. The drawbridge is bigger than the doorway and could never be raised.
12. The boat has a motor—something not even rich guys like Rapunzel's dad could have ever owned at the time.
13. The artist spelled his own name wrong.

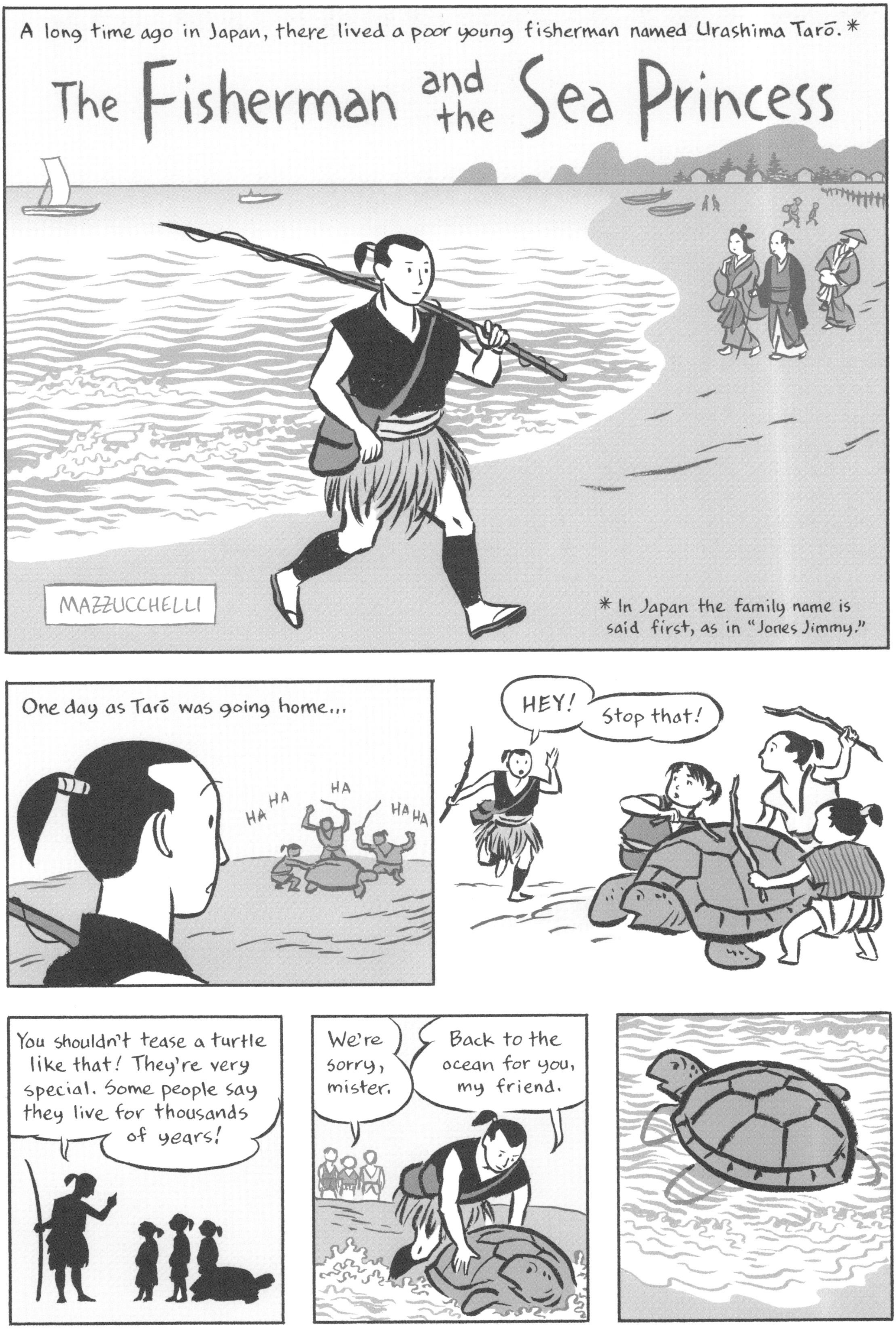
A long time ago in Japan, there lived a poor young fisherman named Urashima Tarō.*
The Fisherman and the Sea Princess
MAZZUCCHELLI
* In Japan the family name is said first, as in "Jones Jimmy."
One day as Tarō was going home...
HA HA
HA
HA HA
HEY!
Stop that!
You shouldn't tease a turtle like that! They're very special. Some people say they live for thousands of years!
We're sorry, mister.
Back to the ocean for you, my friend.

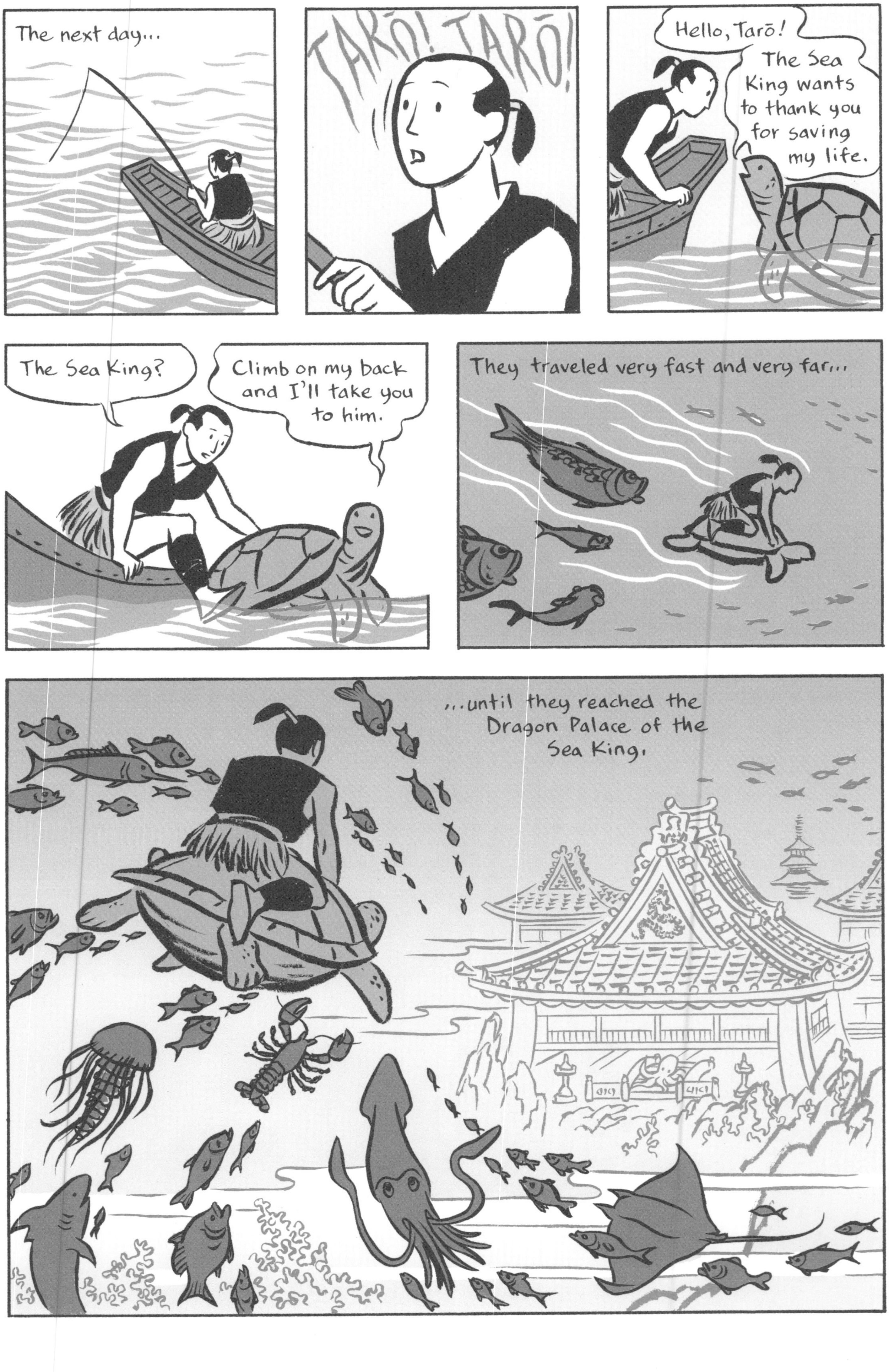
The next day...
TARŌ! TARŌ!
Hello, Tarō!
The Sea King wants to thank you for saving my life.
The Sea King?
Climb on my back and I'll take you to him.
They traveled very fast and very far...
...until they reached the Dragon Palace of the Sea King.

little

LIT

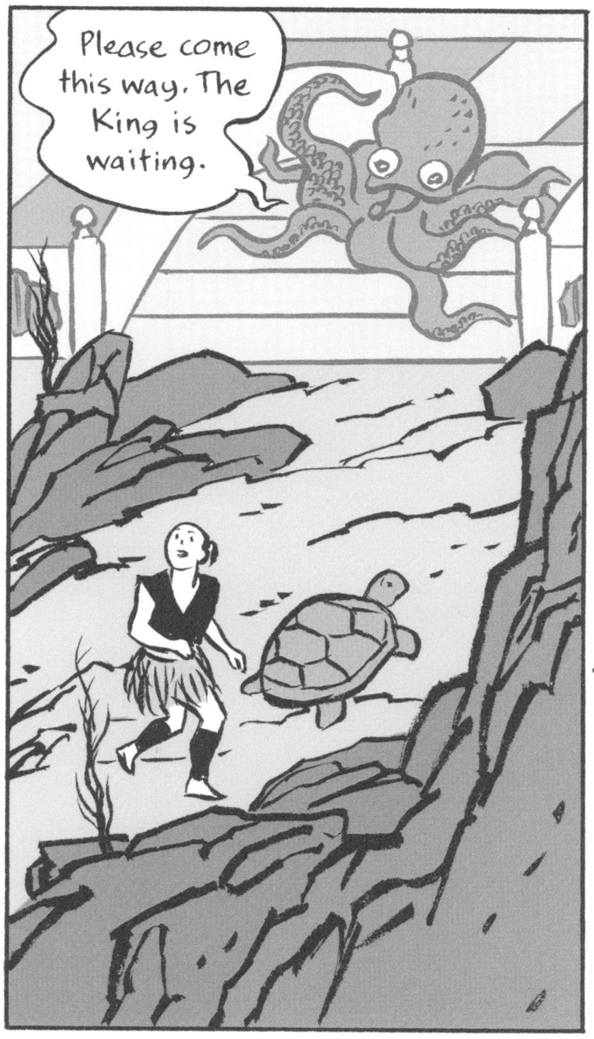
Please come this way. The King is waiting.

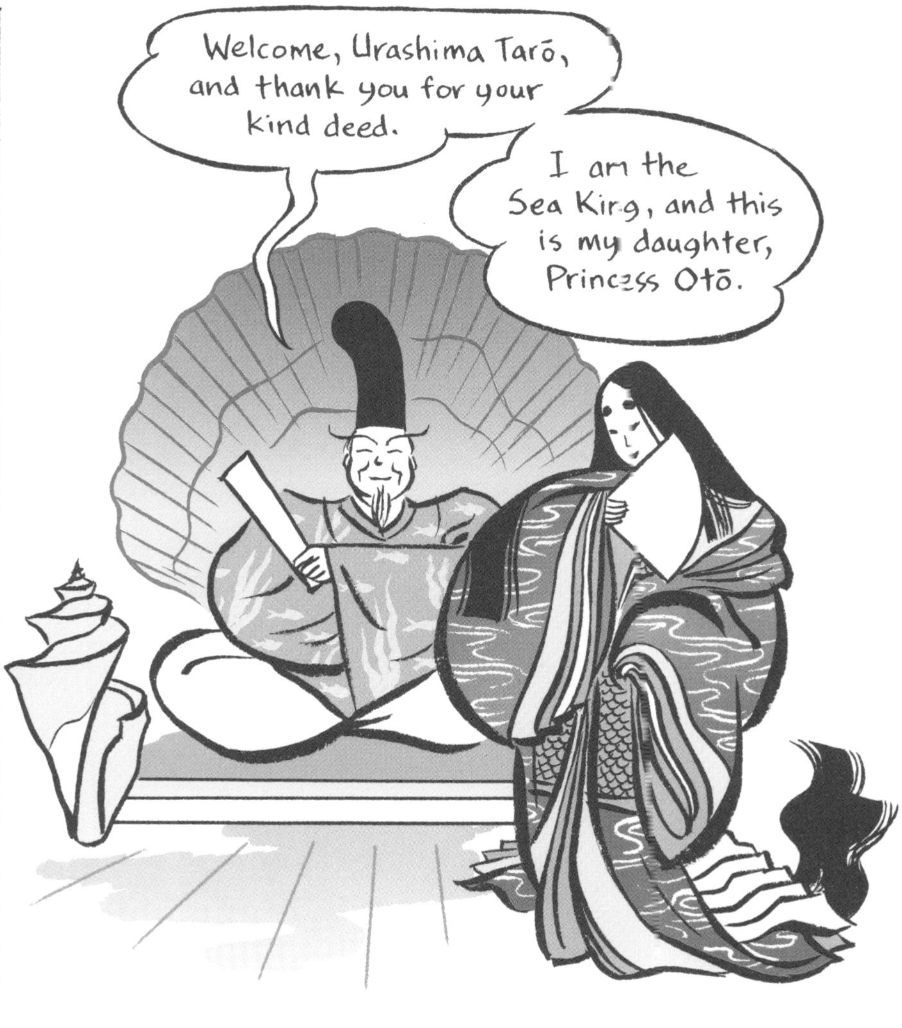
Welcome, Urashima Tarō, and thank you for your kind deed.
I am the Sea King, and this is my daughter, Princess Otō.

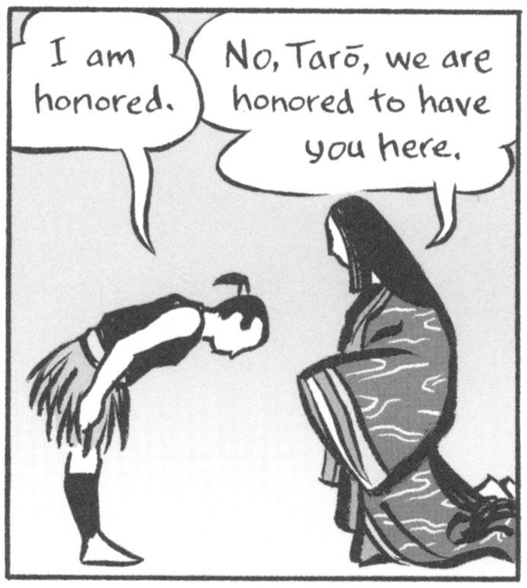
I am honored.
No, Tarō, we are honored to have you here.

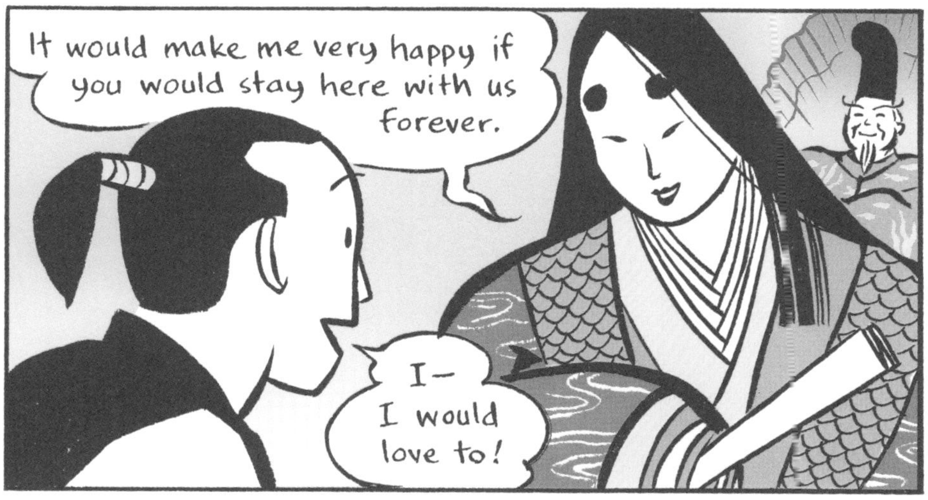
It would make me very happy if you would stay here with us forever.
I— I would love to!

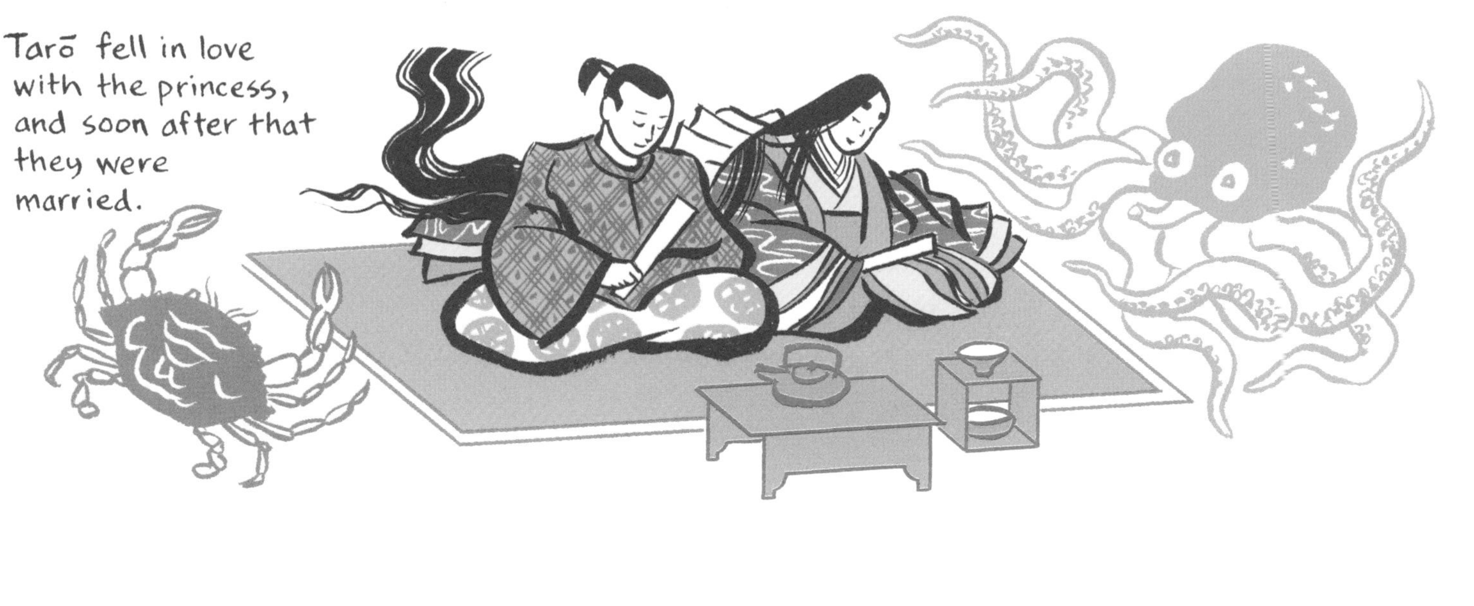
Tarō fell in love with the princess, and soon after that they were married.

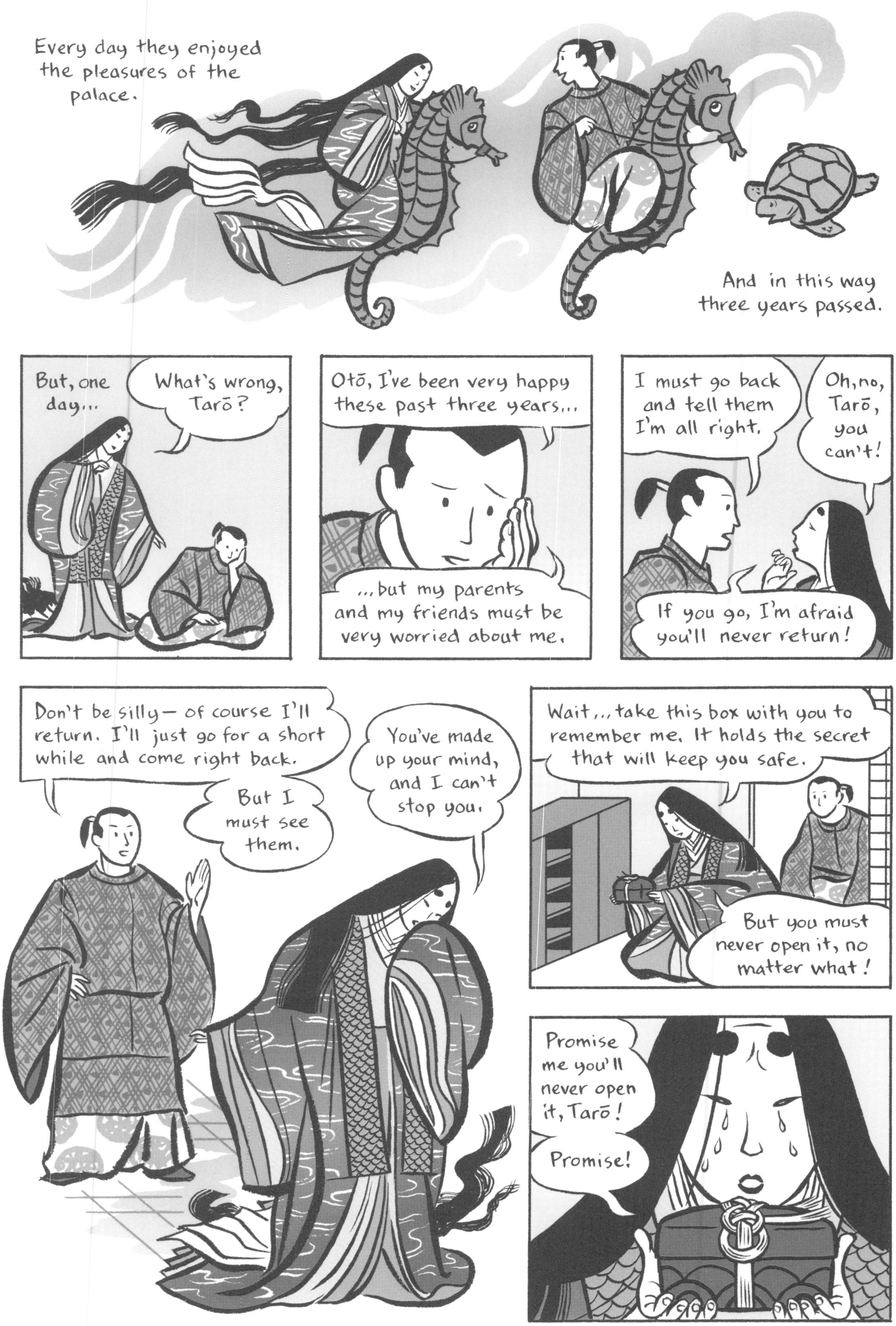
Every day they enjoyed the pleasures of the palace.
And in this way three years passed.
But, one day...
What's wrong, Tarō?
Otō, I've been very happy these past three years...
...but my parents and my friends must be very worried about me.
I must go back and tell them I'm all right.
Oh, no, Tarō, you can't!
If you go, I'm afraid you'll never return!
Don't be silly— of course I'll return. I'll just go for a short while and come right back.
But I must see them.
You've made up your mind, and I can't stop you.
Wait... take this box with you to remember me. It holds the secret that will keep you safe.
But you must never open it, no matter what!
Promise me you'll never open it, Tarō!
Promise!

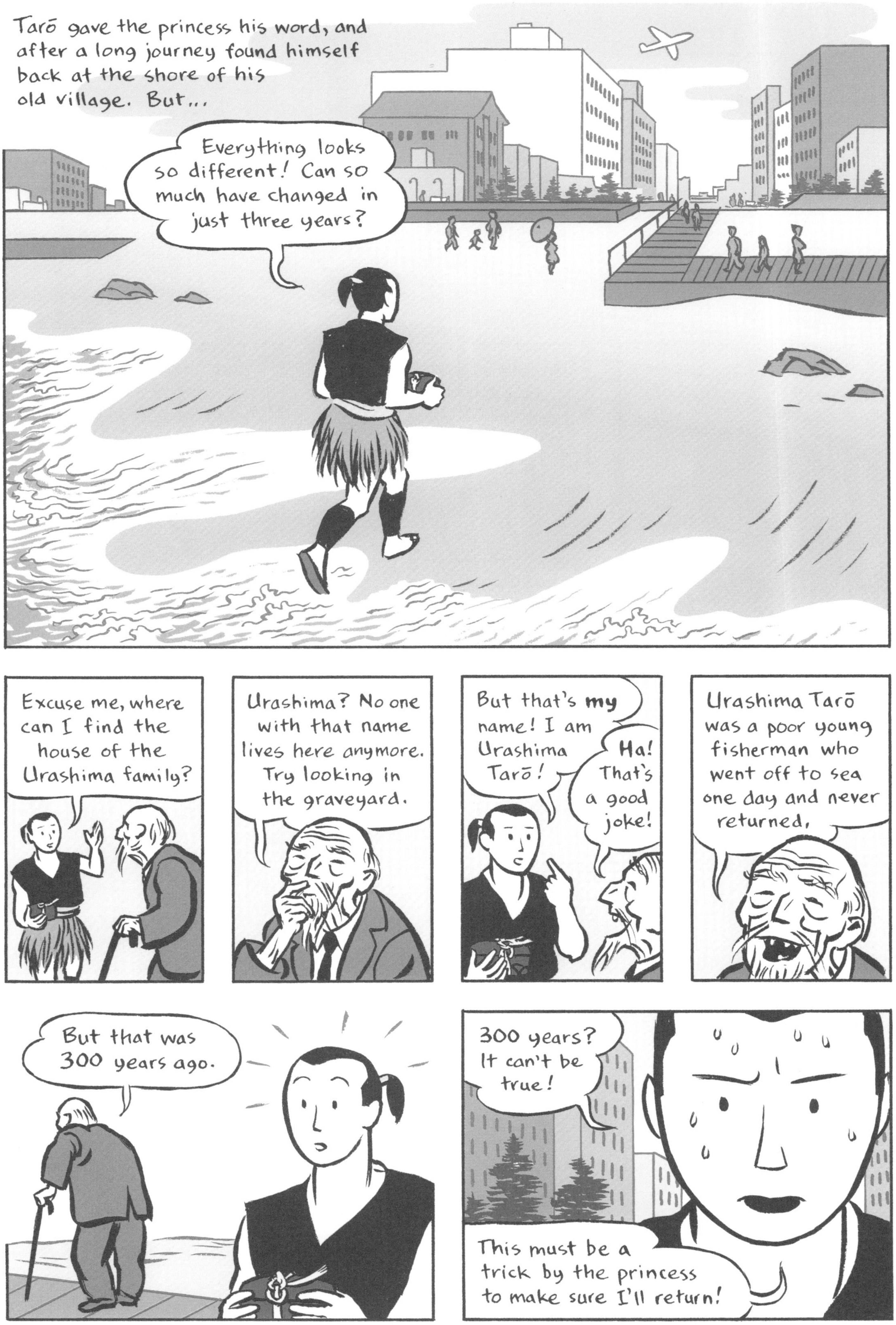
Tarō gave the princess his word, and after a long journey found himself back at the shore of his old village. But...
Everything looks so different! Can so much have changed in just three years?
Excuse me, where can I find the house of the Urashima family?
Urashima? No one with that name lives here anymore. Try looking in the graveyard.
But that's **my** name! I am Urashima Tarō!
Ha! That's a good joke!
Urashima Tarō was a poor young fisherman who went off to sea one day and never returned,
But that was 300 years ago.
300 years? It can't be true!
This must be a trick by the princess to make sure I'll return!

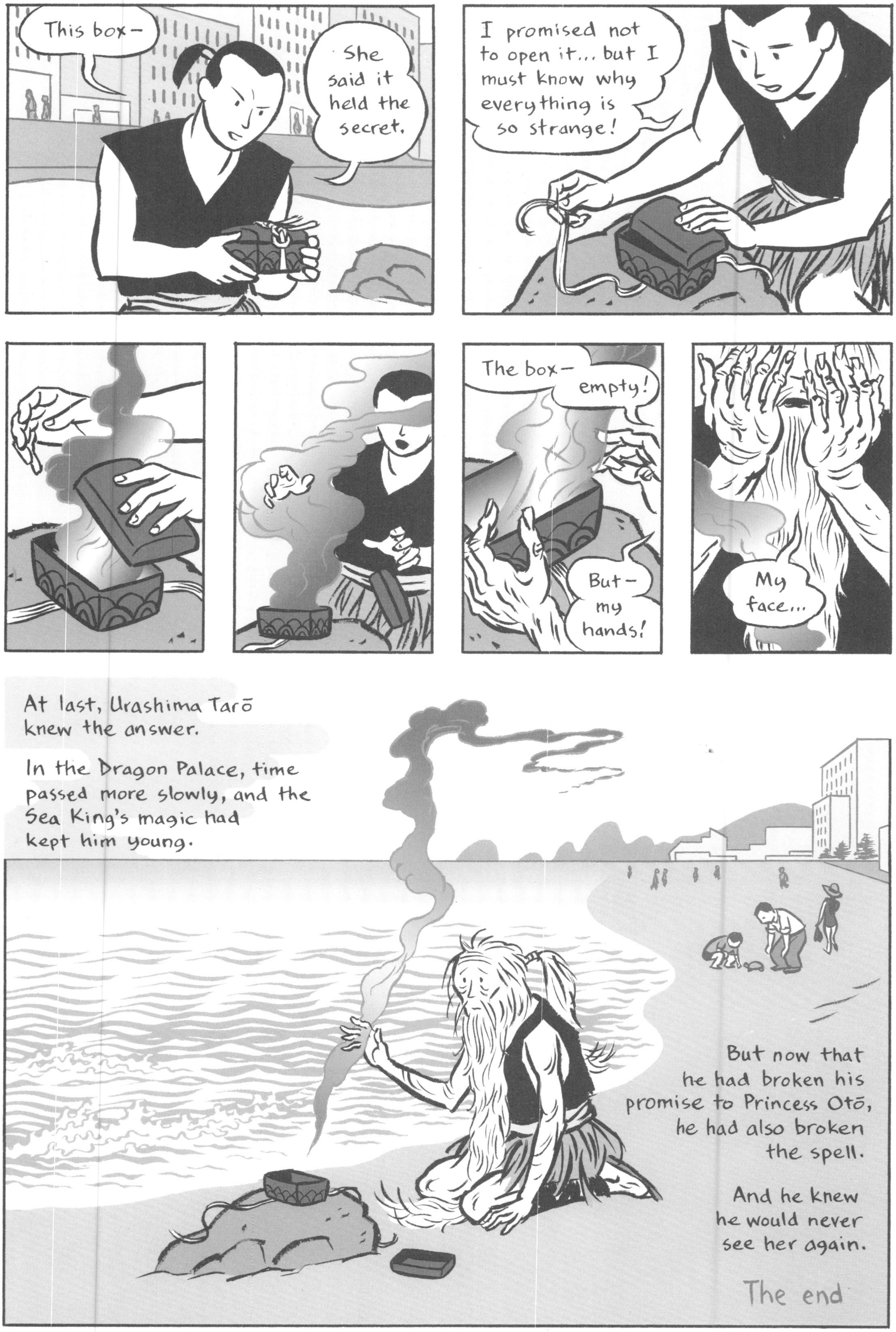
This box—
She said it held the secret.
I promised not to open it... but I must know why everything is so strange!
The box—
empty!
But—my hands!
My face...
At last, Urashima Tarō knew the answer.
In the Dragon Palace, time passed more slowly, and the Sea King's magic had kept him young.
But now that he had broken his promise to Princess Otō, he had also broken the spell.
And he knew he would never see her again.
The end

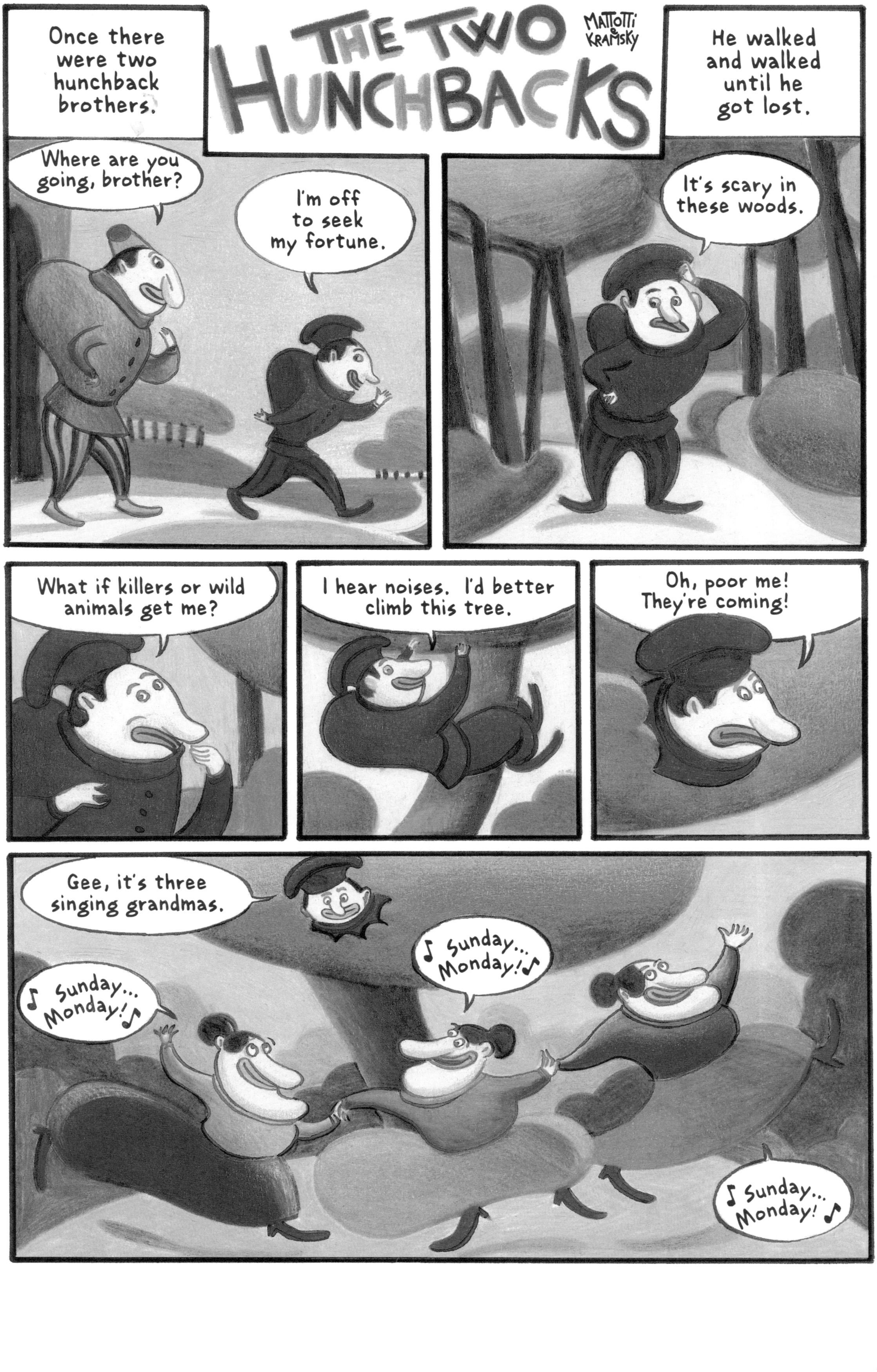
Once there were two hunchback brothers.
THE TWO HUNCHBACKS
MATTOTTI & KRAMSKY
He walked and walked until he got lost.
Where are you going, brother?
I'm off to seek my fortune.
It's scary in these woods.
What if killers or wild animals get me?
I hear noises. I'd better climb this tree.
Oh, poor me! They're coming!
Gee, it's three singing grandmas.
♪ Sunday... Monday! ♪
♪ Sunday... Monday! ♪
♪ Sunday... Monday! ♪

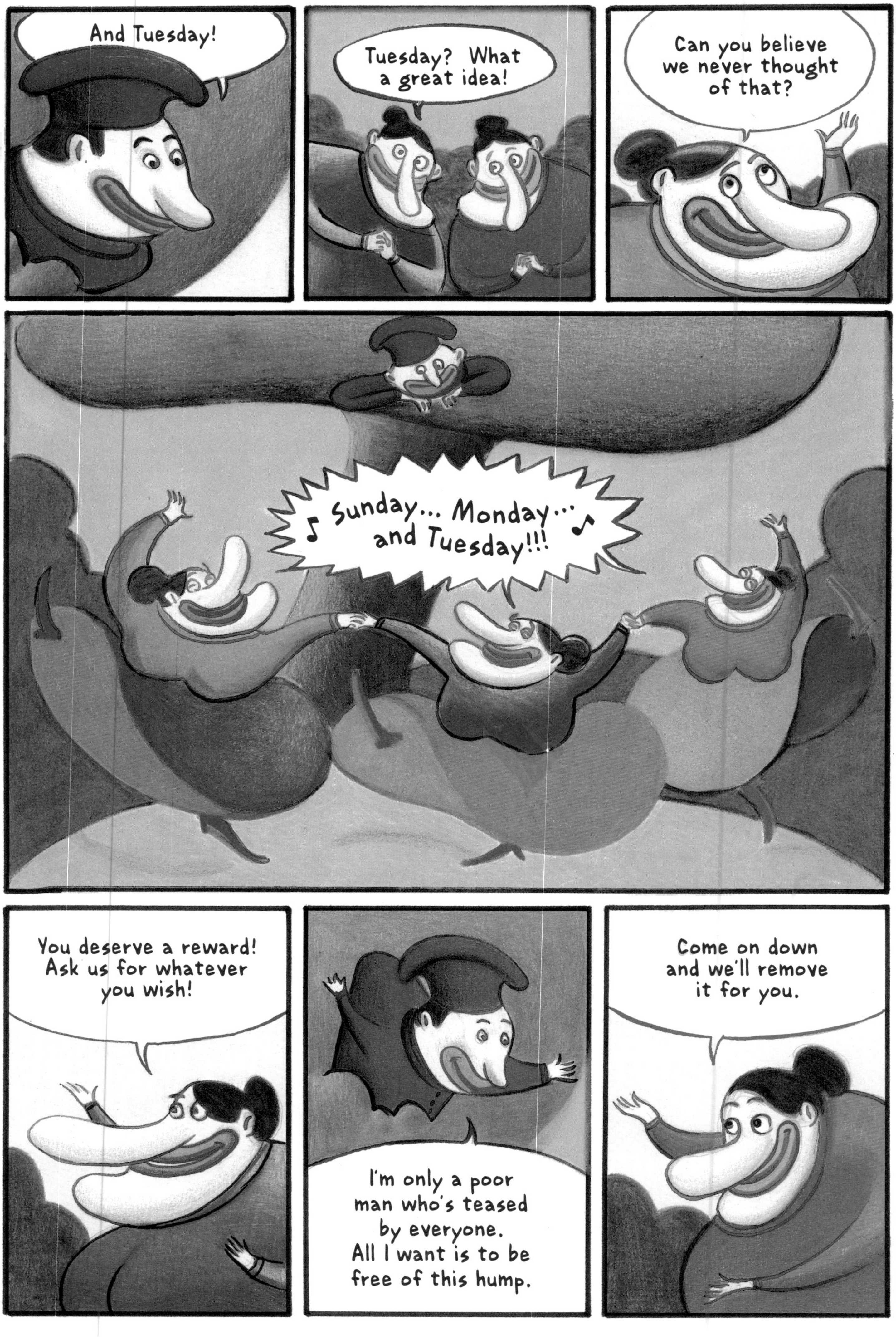
And Tuesday!
Tuesday? What a great idea!
Can you believe we never thought of that?
Sunday... Monday... and Tuesday!!!
You deserve a reward! Ask us for whatever you wish!
I'm only a poor man who's teased by everyone. All I want is to be free of this hump.
Come on down and we'll remove it for you.

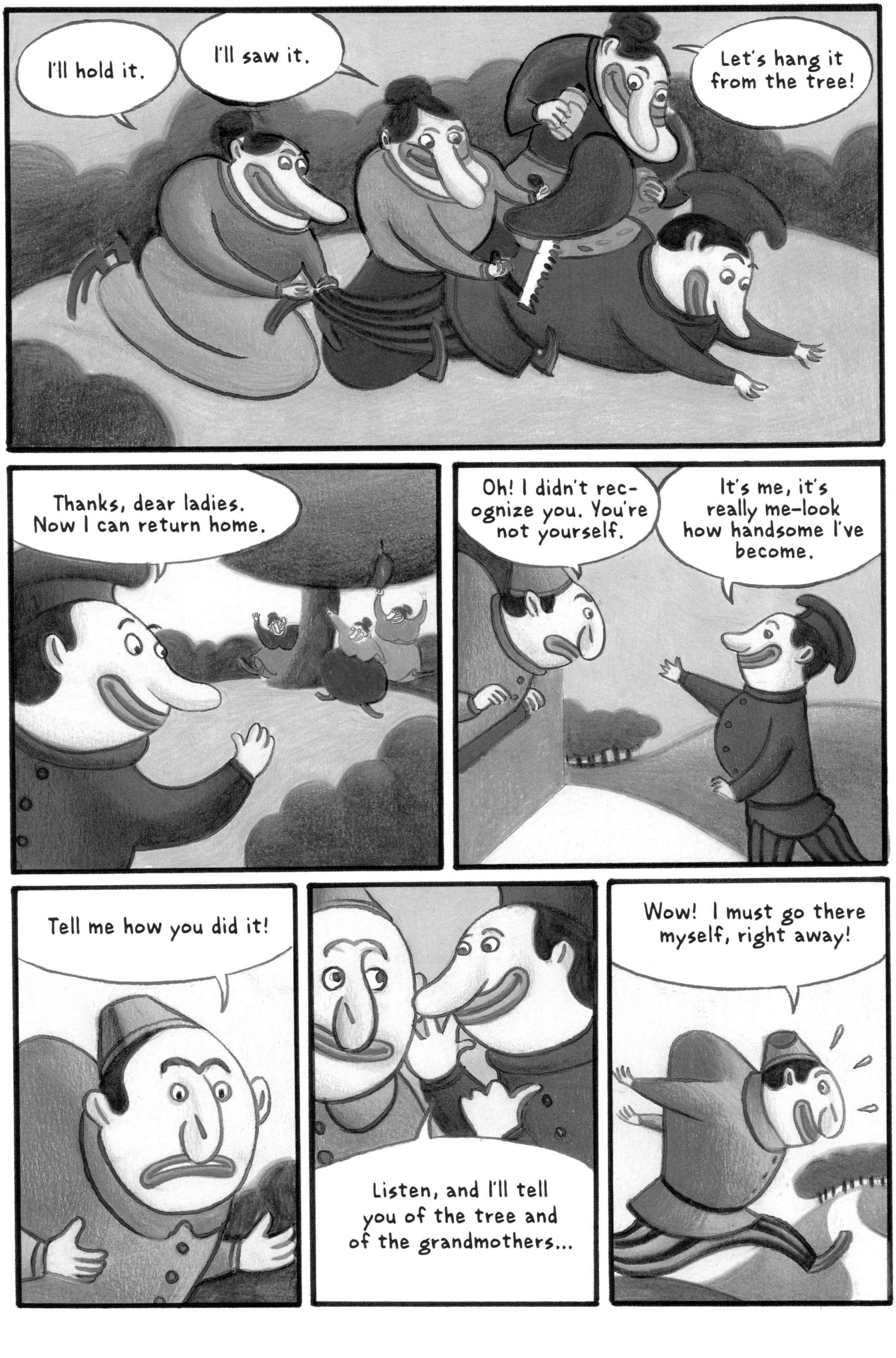
I'll hold it.
I'll saw it.
Let's hang it from the tree!
Thanks, dear ladies. Now I can return home.
Oh! I didn't recognize you. You're not yourself.
It's me, it's really me–look how handsome I've become.
Tell me how you did it!
Listen, and I'll tell you of the tree and of the grandmothers...
Wow! I must go there myself, right away!

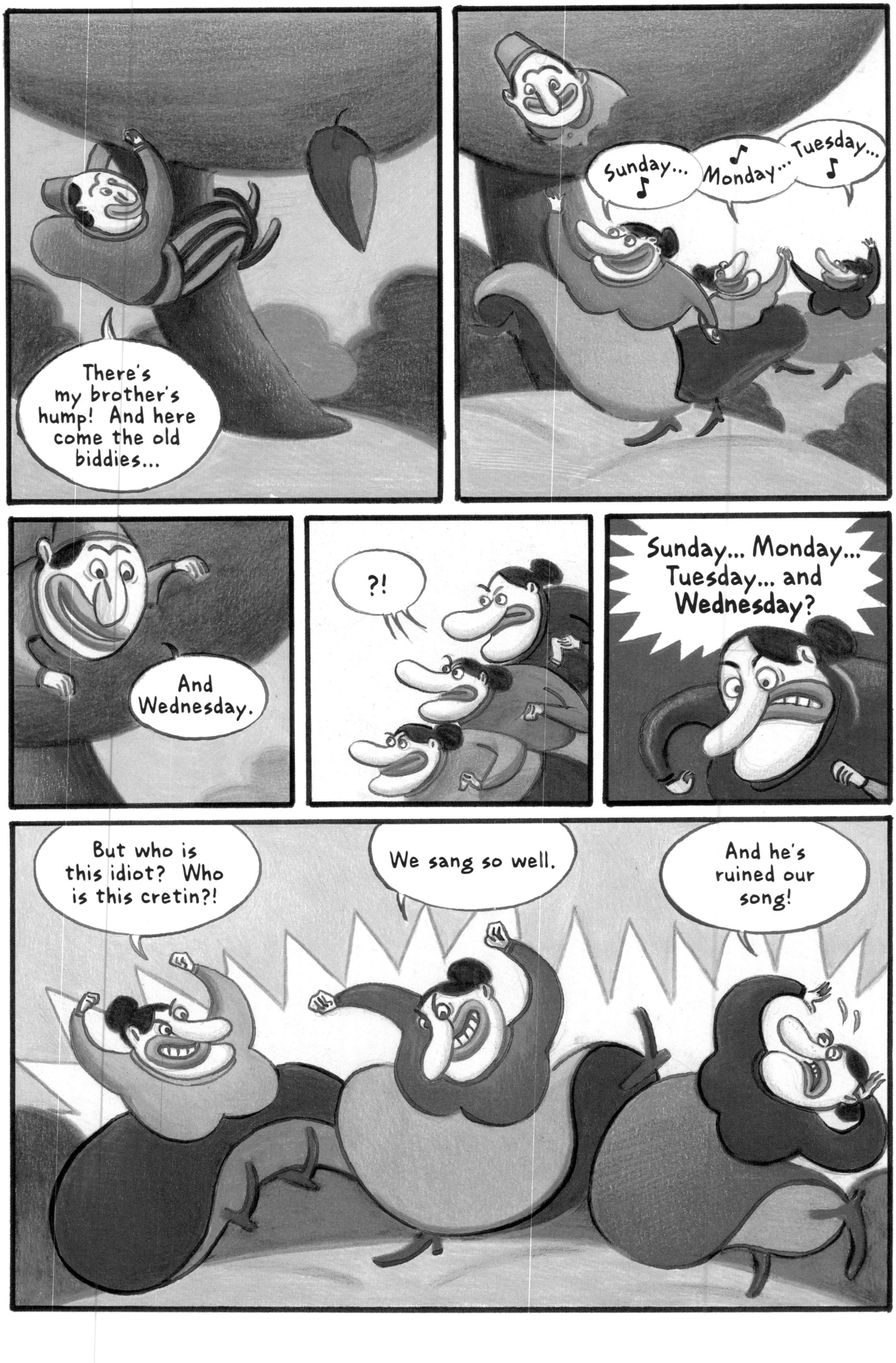
There's my brother's hump! And here come the old biddies...
Sunday... ♪
♪ Monday...
Tuesday... ♪
And Wednesday.
?!
Sunday... Monday... Tuesday... and Wednesday?
But who is this idiot? Who is this cretin?!
We sang so well.
And he's ruined our song!

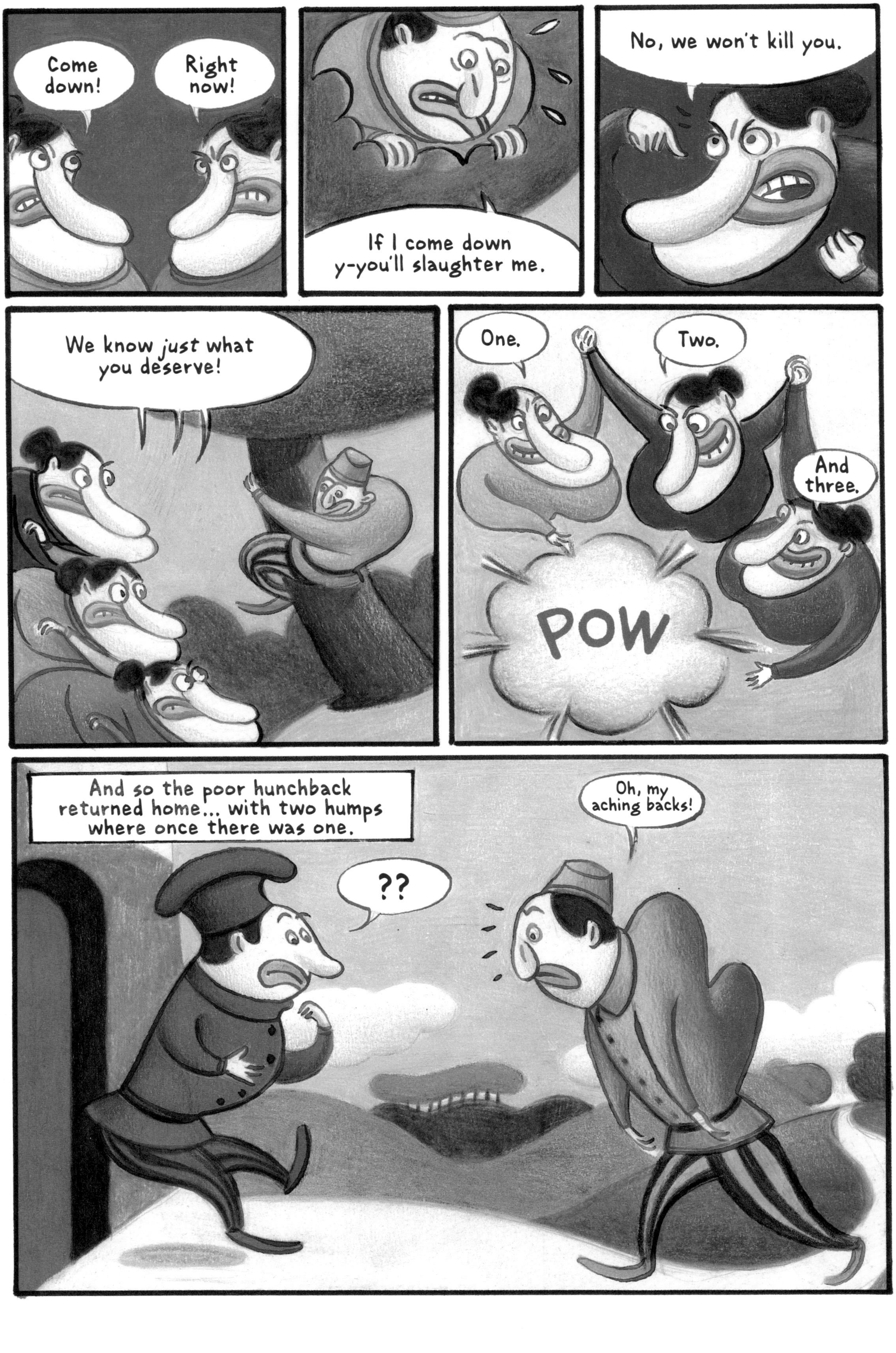
Come down!
Right now!
If I come down y-you'll slaughter me.
No, we won't kill you.
We know *just* what you deserve!
One.
Two.
And three.
POW
And so the poor hunchback returned home... with two humps where once there was one.
??
Oh, my aching backs!

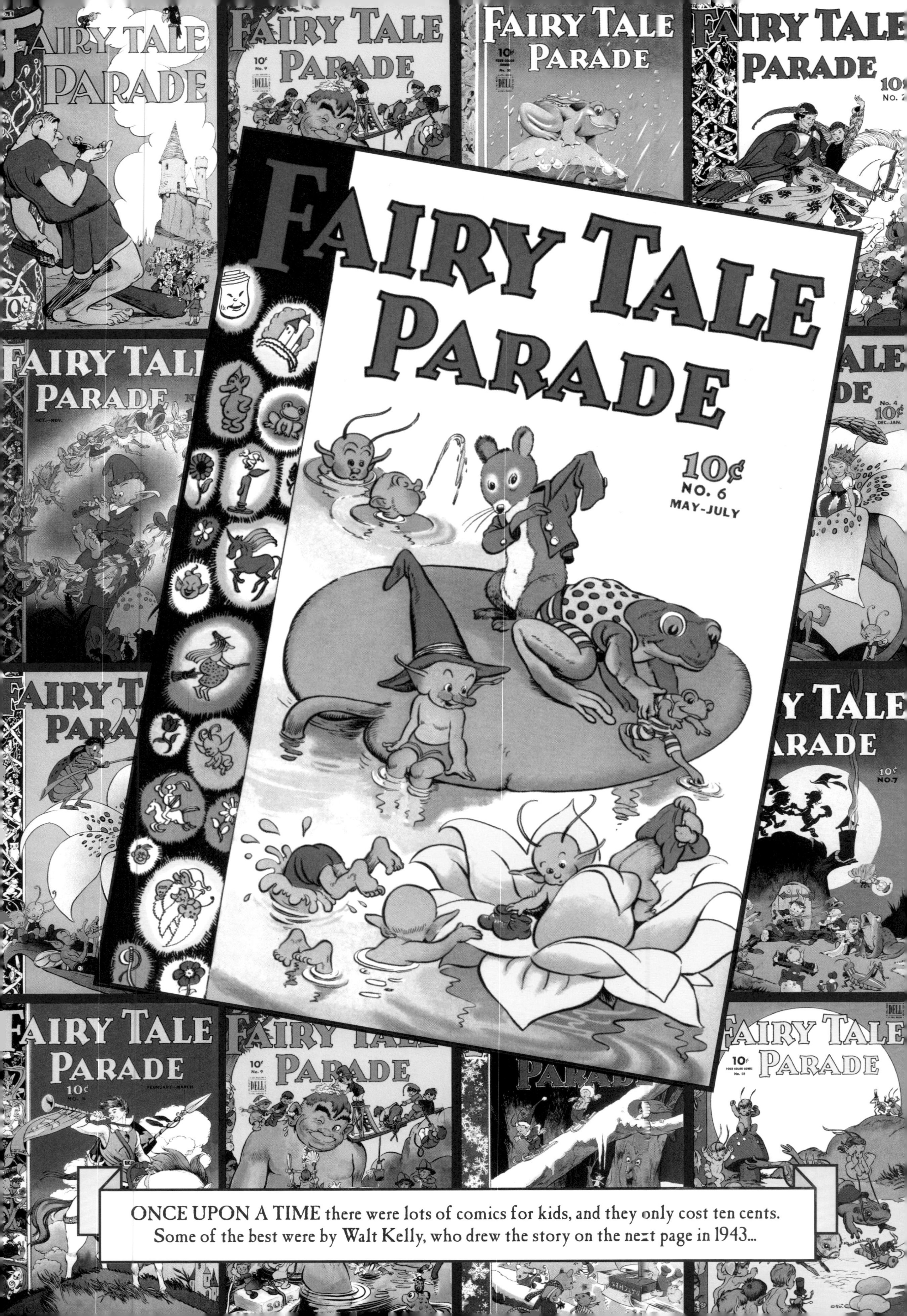
FAIRY TALE PARADE
10¢
NO. 6
MAY-JULY

ONCE UPON A TIME there were lots of comics for kids, and they only cost ten cents. Some of the best were by Walt Kelly, who drew the story on the next page in 1943...

The GINGERBREAD Man

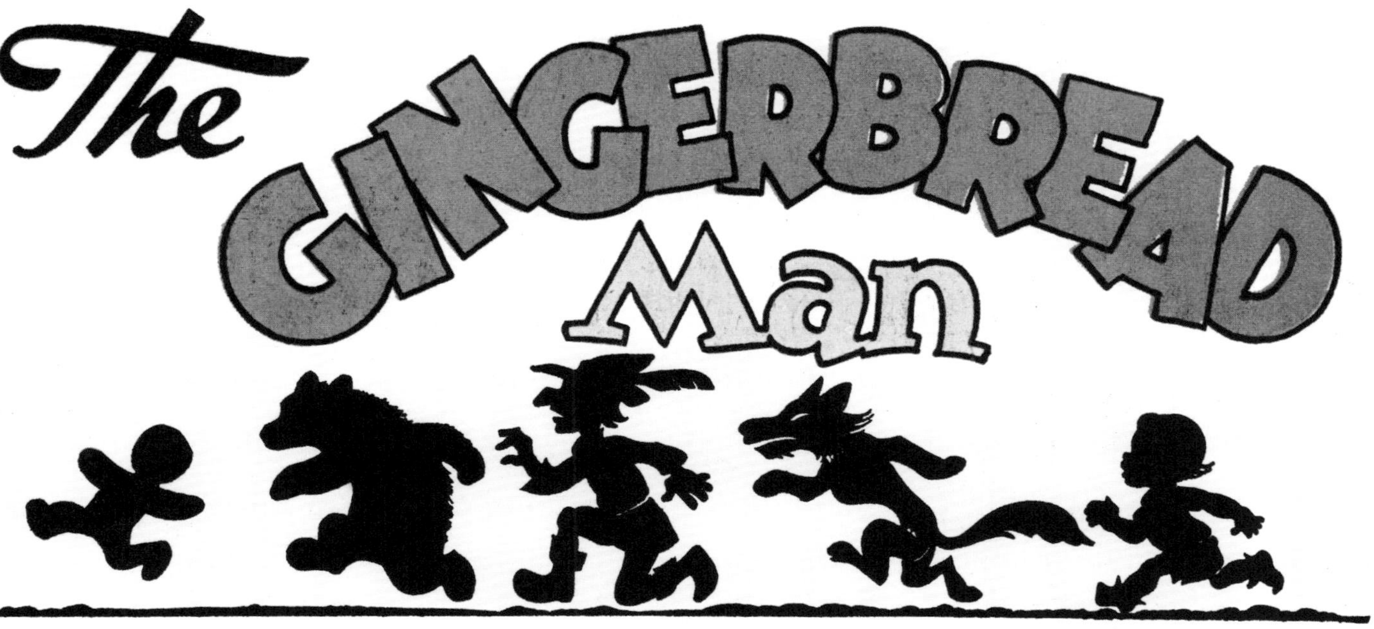

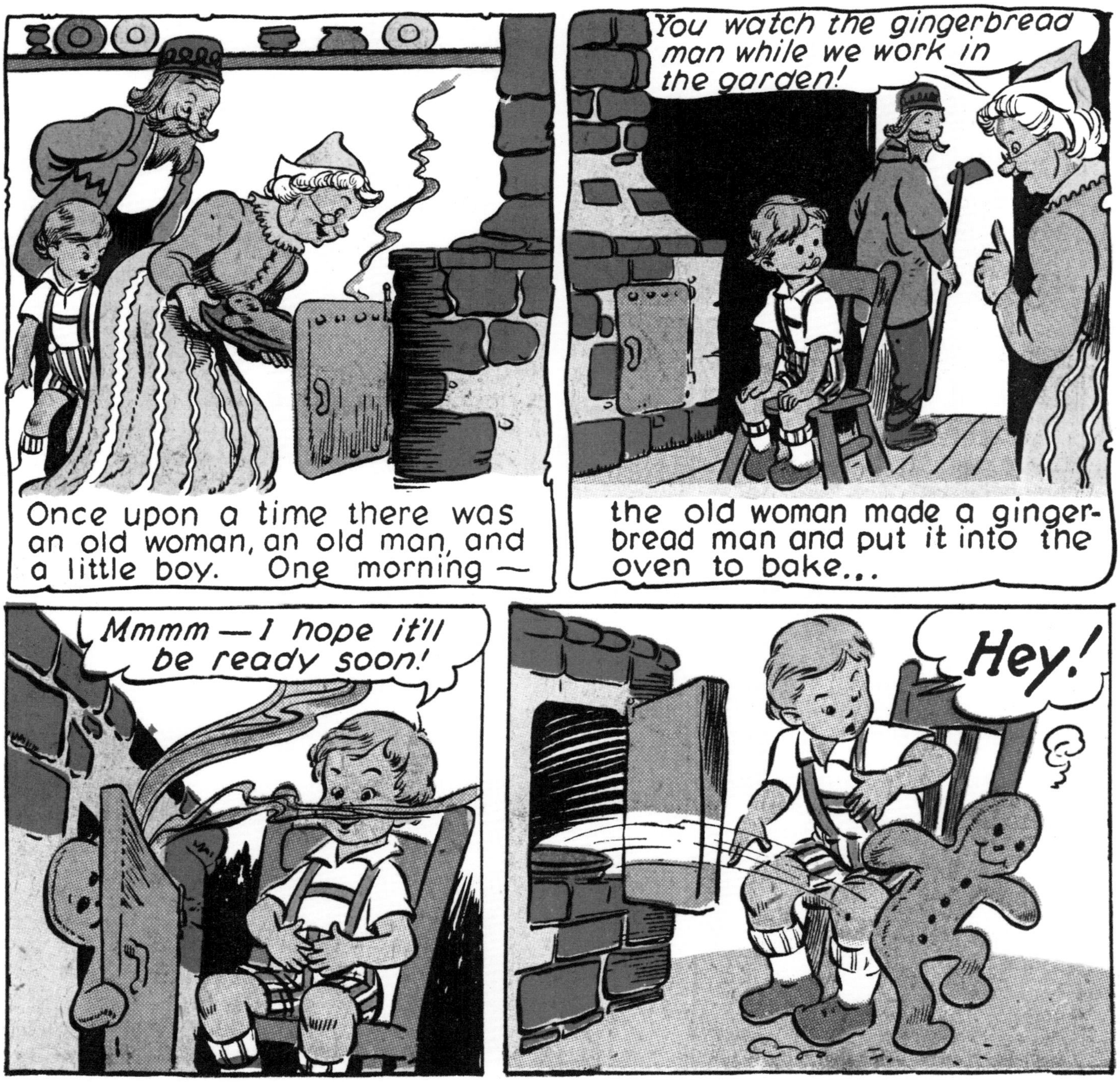
Once upon a time there was an old woman, an old man, and a little boy. One morning —
You watch the gingerbread man while we work in the garden!
the old woman made a gingerbread man and put it into the oven to bake...
Mmmm — I hope it'll be ready soon!
Hey!

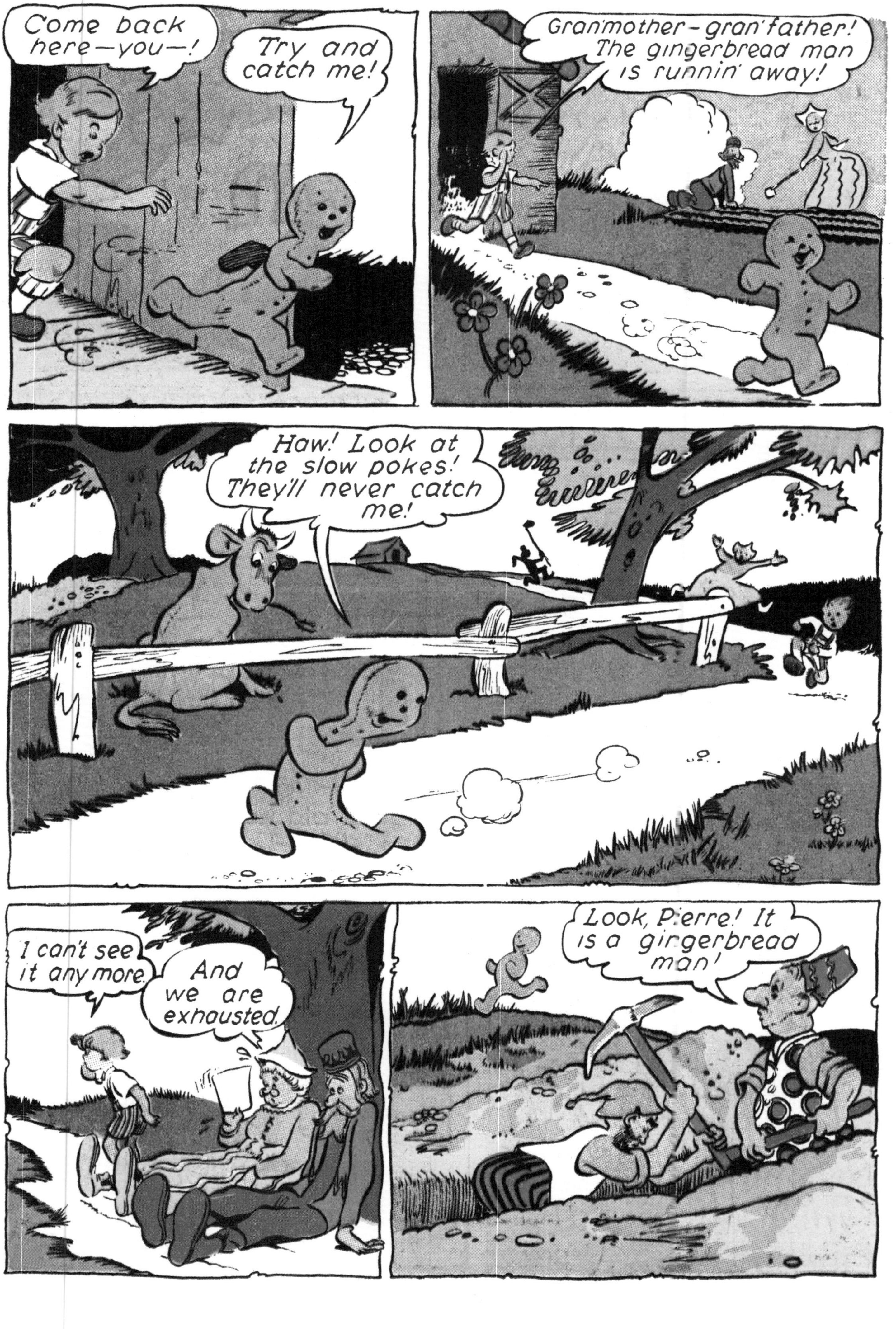
Come back here—you—!
Try and catch me!
Gran'mother - gran'father! The gingerbread man is runnin' away!
Haw! Look at the slow pokes! They'll never catch me!
I can't see it any more.
And we are exhausted.
Look, Pierre! It is a girgerbread man!

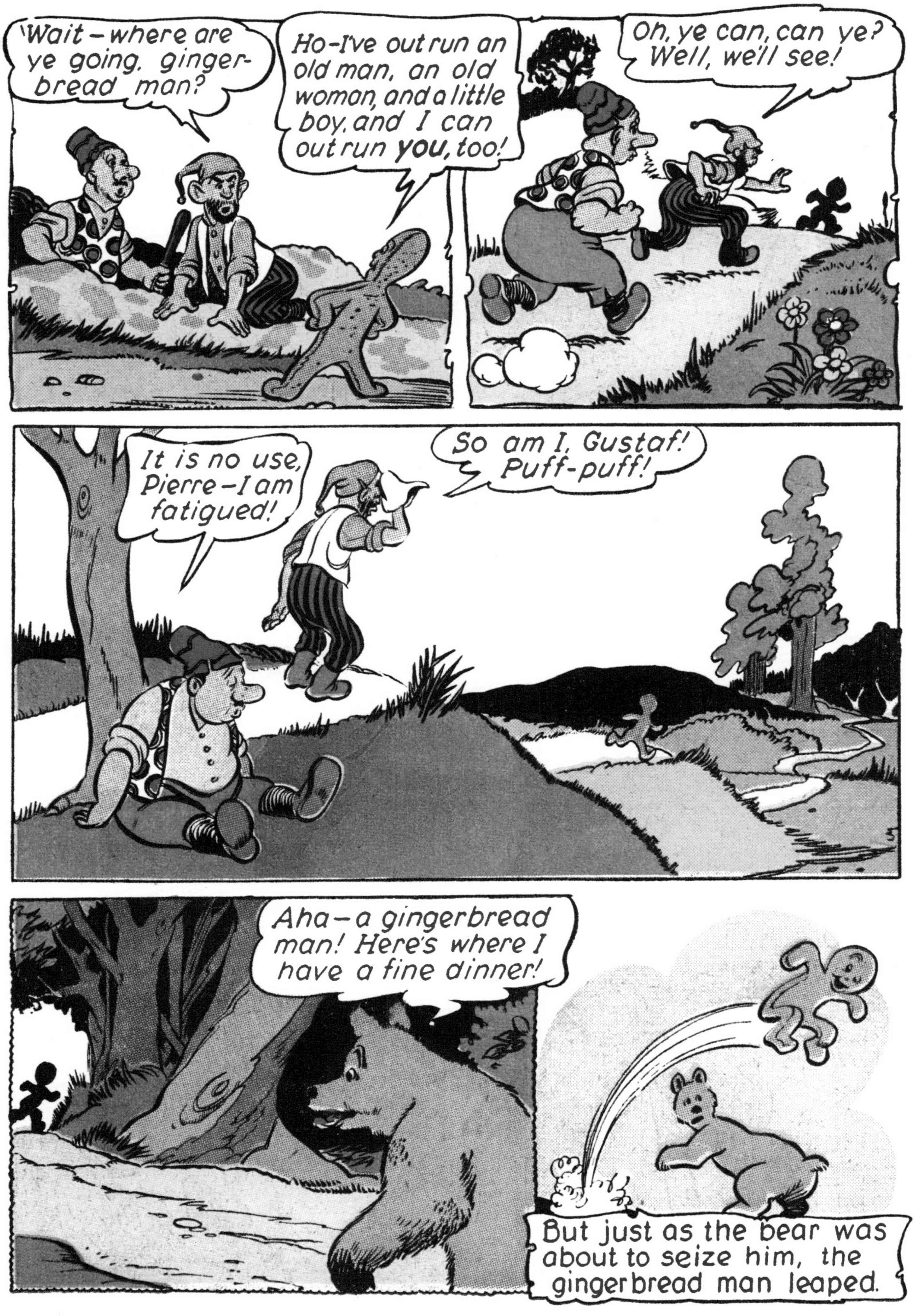

'Wait—where are ye going, ginger-bread man?
Ho-I've outrun an old man, an old woman, and a little boy, and I can outrun **YOU**, too!
Oh, ye can, can ye? Well, we'll see!
It is no use, Pierre—I am fatigued!
So am I, Gustaf! Puff-puff!
Aha—a gingerbread man! Here's where I have a fine dinner!
But just as the bear was about to seize him, the gingerbread man leaped.

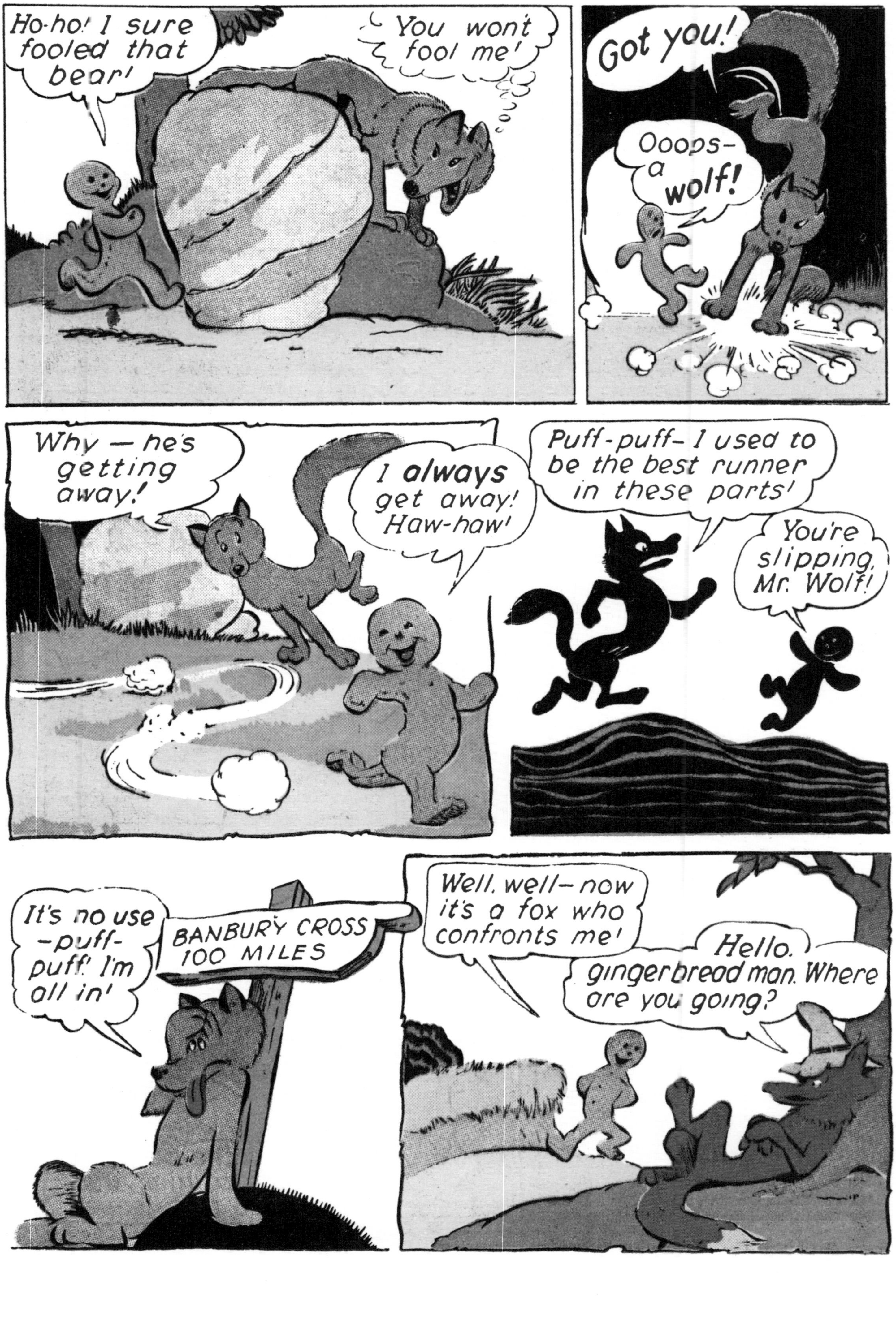
Ho-ho! I sure fooled that bear!
You won't fool me!
Got you!
Ooops- a wolf!
Why — he's getting away!
I always get away! Haw-haw!
Puff-puff- I used to be the best runner in these parts!
You're slipping, Mr. Wolf!
It's no use -puff-puff! I'm all in!
BANBURY CROSS 100 MILES
Well, well- now it's a fox who confronts me!
Hello, gingerbread man. Where are you going?

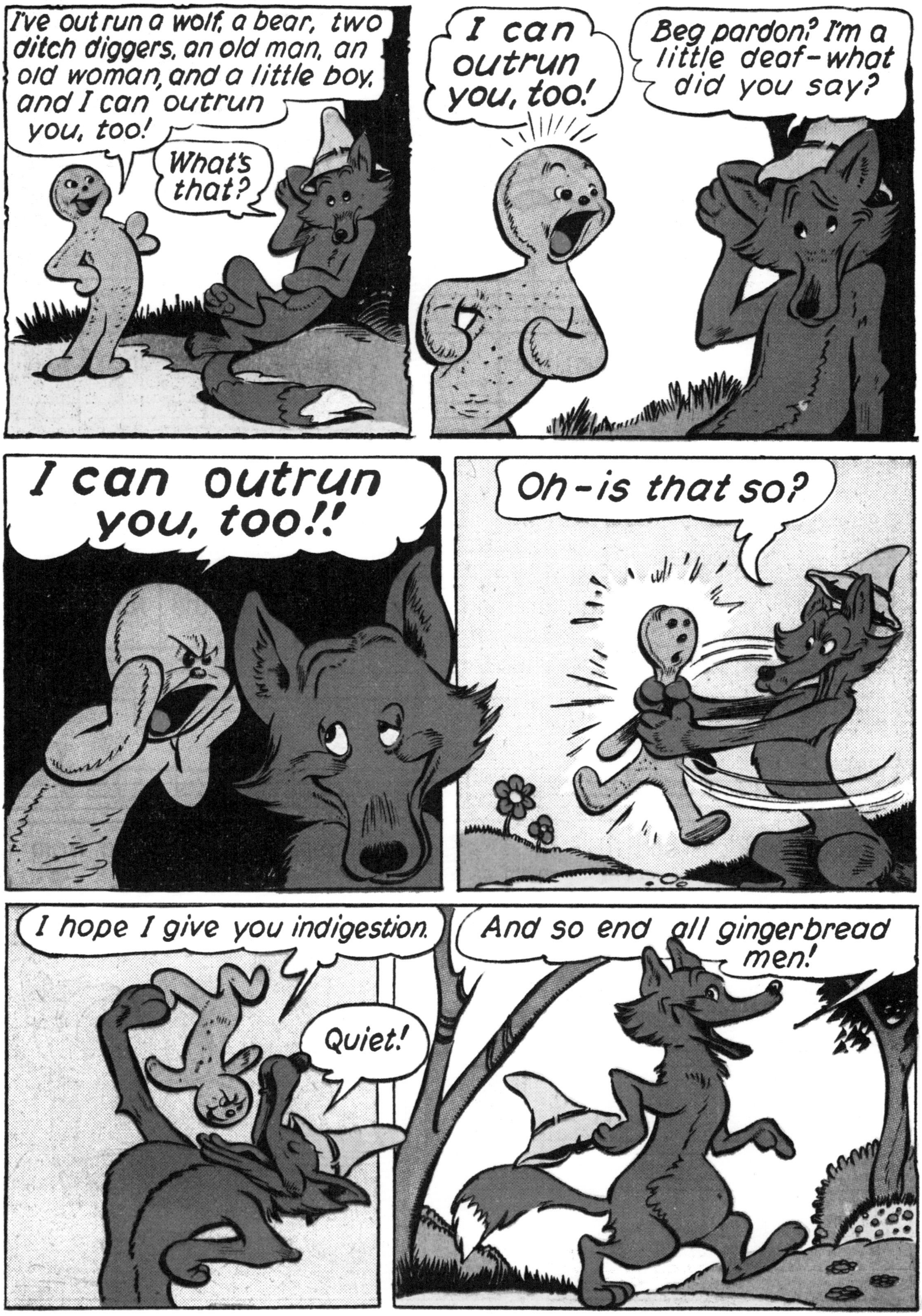
I've outrun a wolf, a bear, two ditch diggers, an old man, an old woman, and a little boy, and I can outrun you, too!
What's that?
I can outrun you, too!
Beg pardon? I'm a little deaf—what did you say?
I can outrun you, too!!
Oh—is that so?
I hope I give you indigestion.
Quiet!
And so end all gingerbread men!

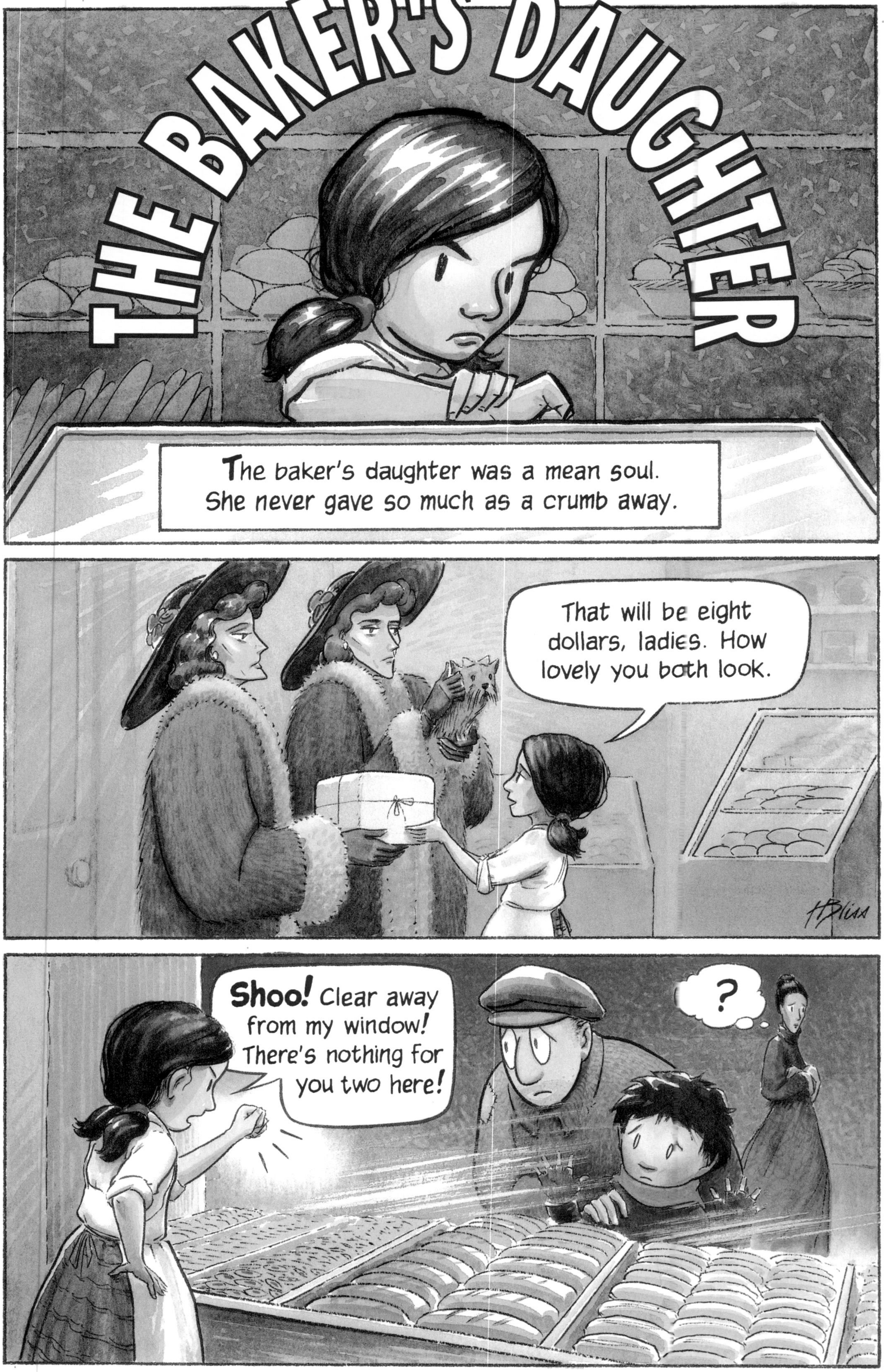
THE BAKER'S DAUGHTER
The baker's daughter was a mean soul. She never gave so much as a crumb away.
That will be eight dollars, ladies. How lovely you both look.
Shoo! Clear away from my window! There's nothing for you two here!
?

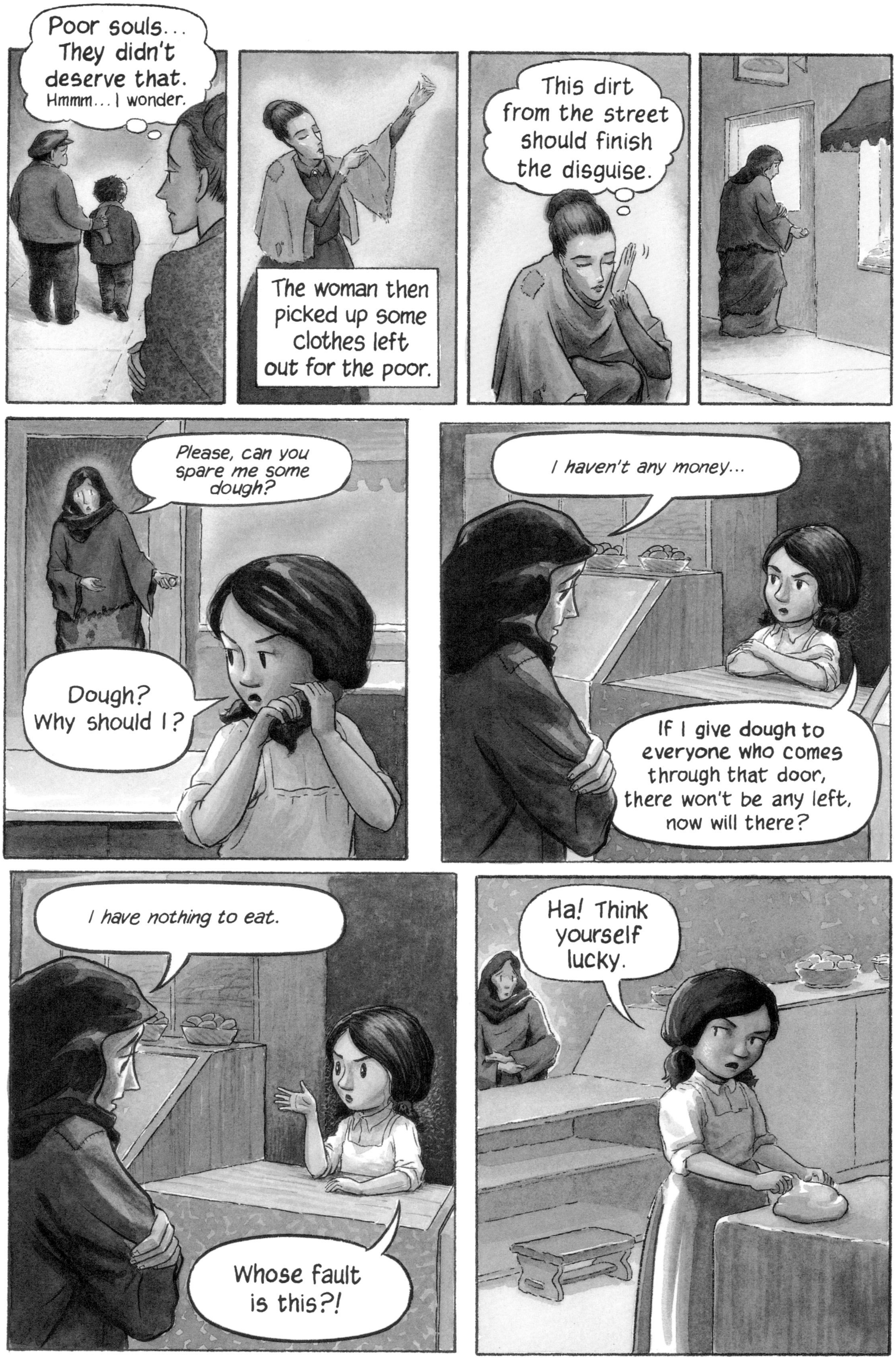
Poor souls... They didn't deserve that. Hmmm... I wonder.
The woman then picked up some clothes left out for the poor.
This dirt from the street should finish the disguise.
Please, can you spare me some dough?
Dough? Why should I?
I haven't any money...
If I give dough to everyone who comes through that door, there won't be any left, now will there?
I have nothing to eat.
Whose fault is this?!
Ha! Think yourself lucky.

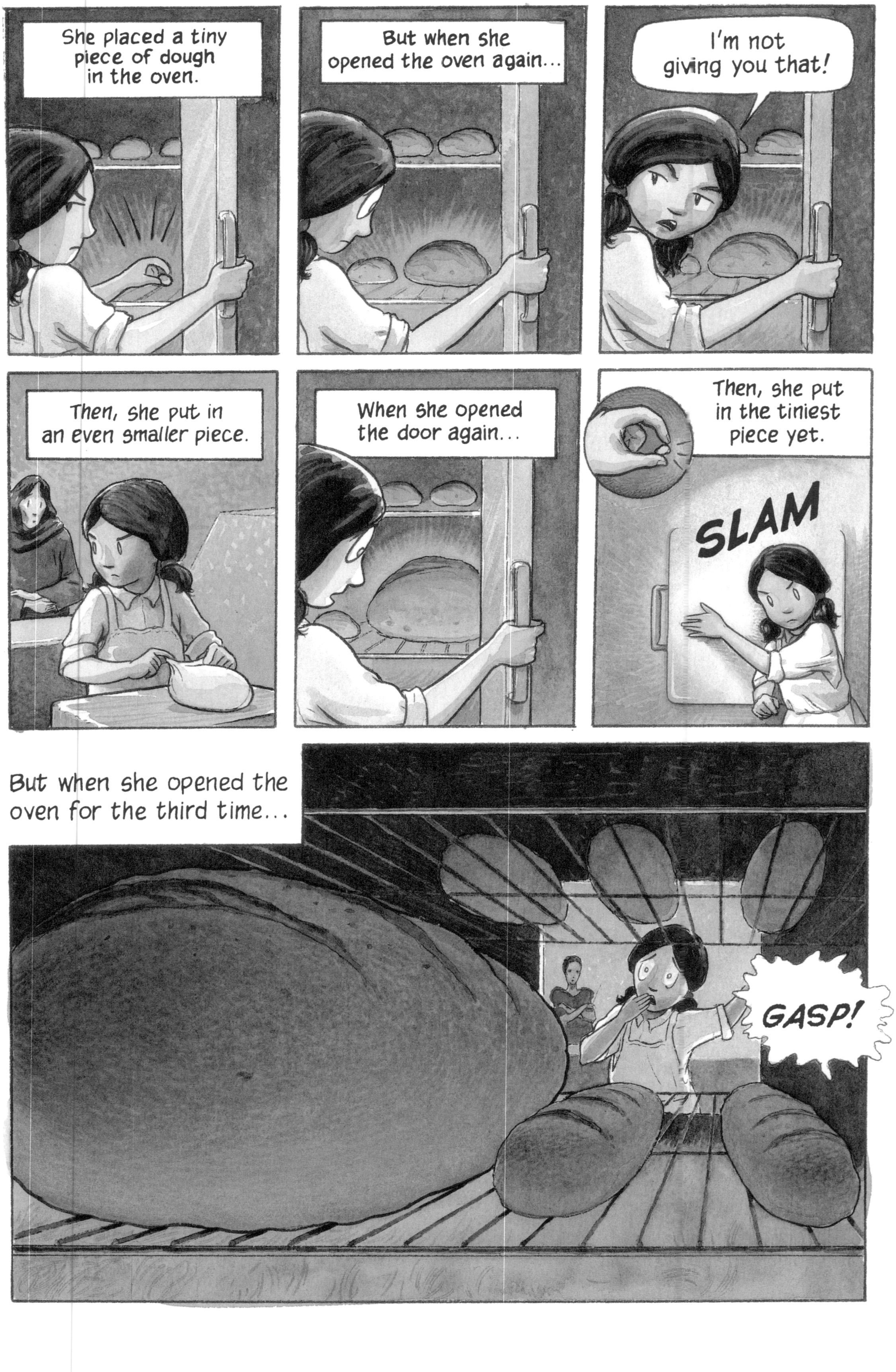
She placed a tiny piece of dough in the oven.
But when she opened the oven again...
I'm not giving you that!
Then, she put in an even smaller piece.
When she opened the door again...
Then, she put in the tiniest piece yet.
SLAM
But when she opened the oven for the third time...
GASP!

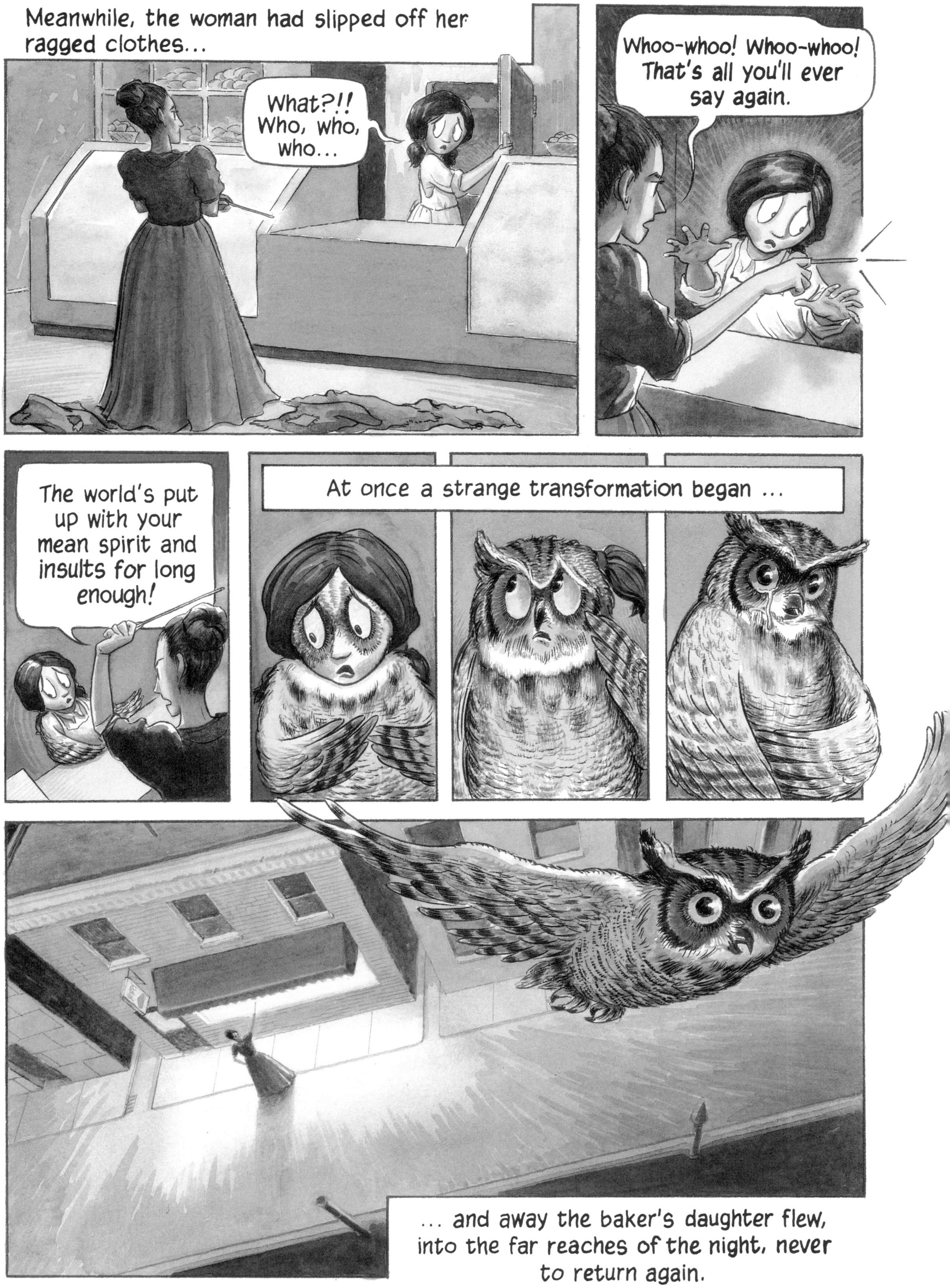
Meanwhile, the woman had slipped off her ragged clothes...
What?!! Who, who, who...
Whoo-whoo! Whoo-whoo! That's all you'll ever say again.
The world's put up with your mean spirit and insults for long enough!
At once a strange transformation began ...
... and away the baker's daughter flew, into the far reaches of the night, never to return again.

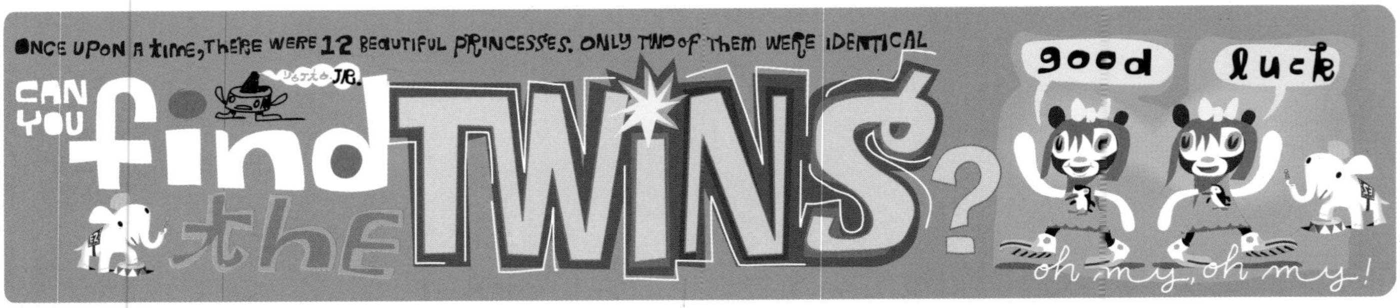
ONCE UPON A TIME, THERE WERE 12 BEAUTIFUL PRINCESSES. ONLY TWO OF THEM WERE IDENTICAL
CAN YOU find the TWINS?
J.B.
good
luck
oh my, oh my!

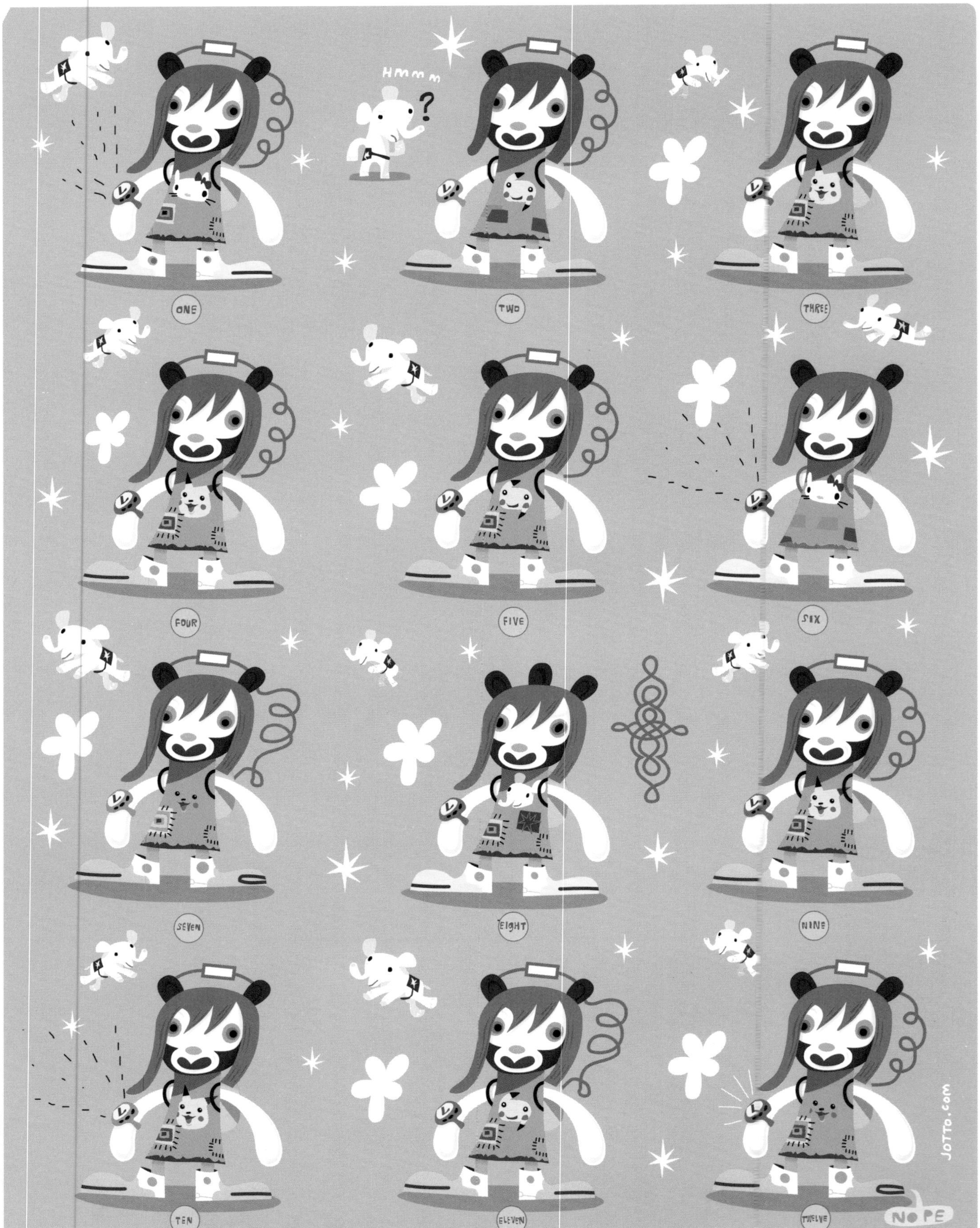
HMMM
?
ONE
TWO
THREE
FOUR
FIVE
SIX
SEVEN
EIGHT
NINE
TEN
ELEVEN
TWELVE
JOTTO.COM
NOPE

the ANSWER IS FOUR and NINE

Jack and his Mom and the Beanstalk

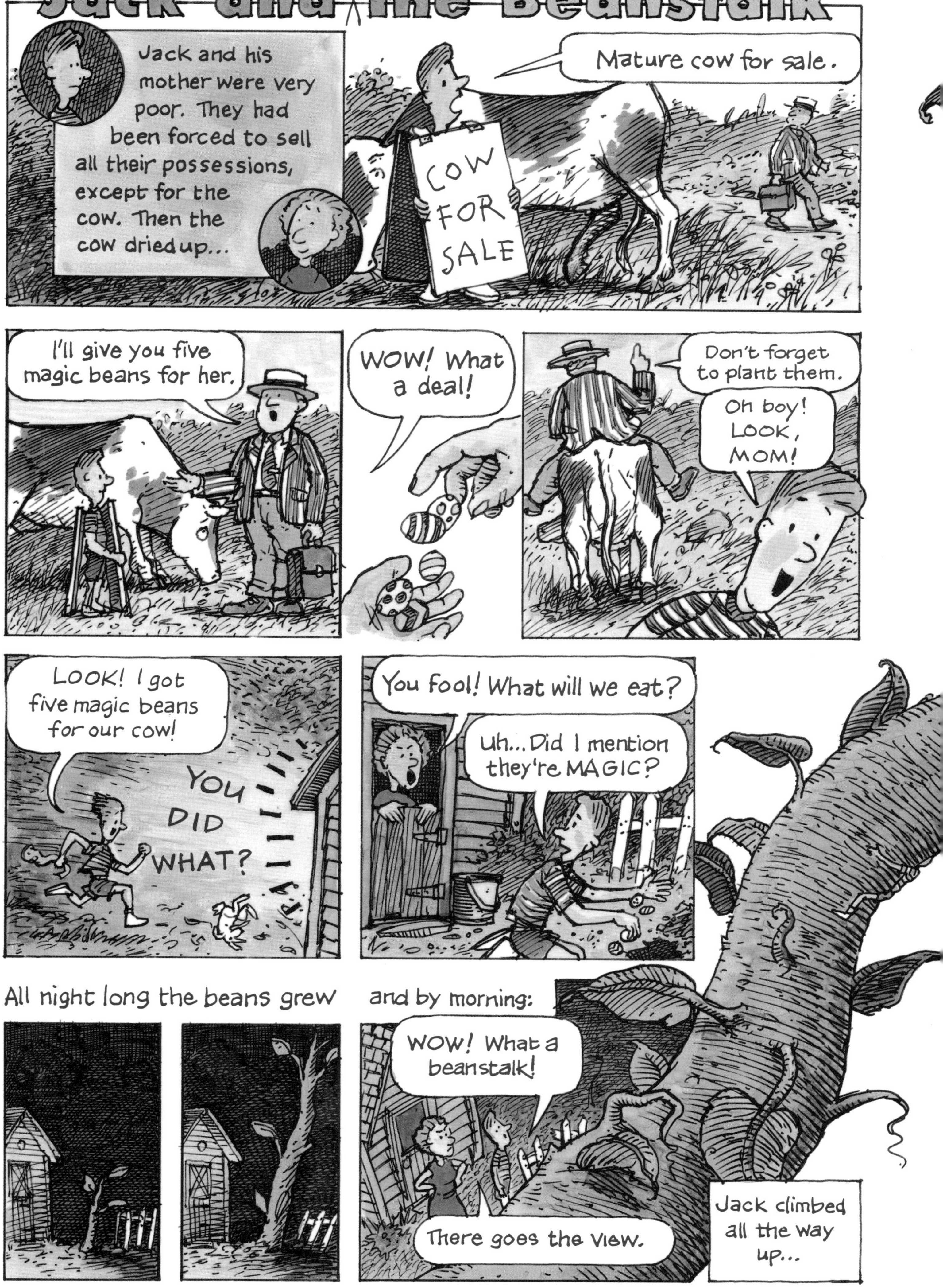
Jack and his mother were very poor. They had been forced to sell all their possessions, except for the cow. Then the cow dried up...
Mature cow for sale.
COW FOR SALE
I'll give you five magic beans for her.
WOW! What a deal!
Don't forget to plant them.
Oh boy! LOOK, MOM!
LOOK! I got five magic beans for our cow!
YOU DID WHAT?
You fool! What will we eat?
Uh... Did I mention they're MAGIC?
All night long the beans grew
and by morning:
WOW! What a beanstalk!
There goes the view.
Jack climbed all the way up...

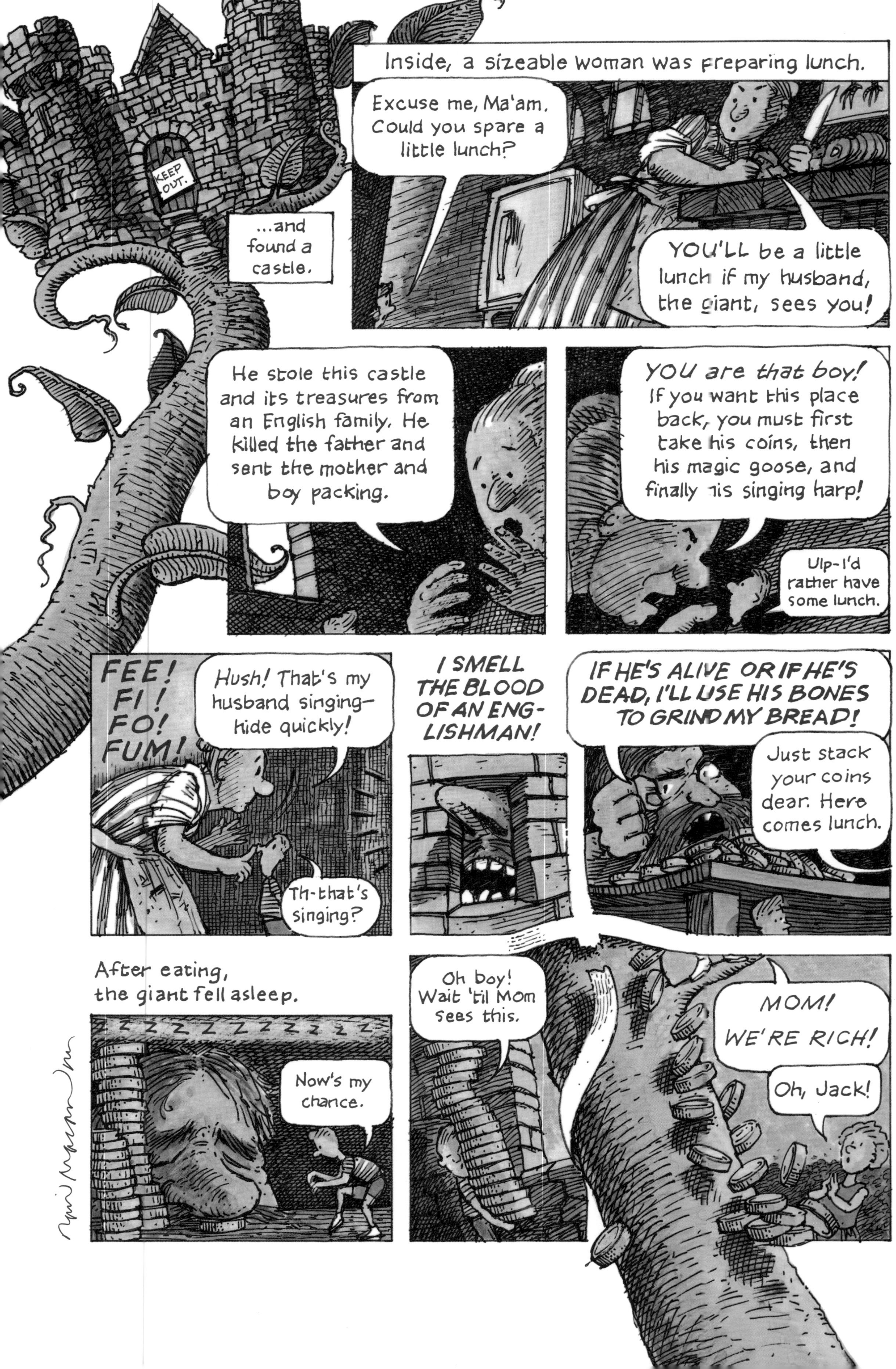
KEEP OUT.
...and found a castle.
Inside, a sizeable woman was preparing lunch.
Excuse me, Ma'am. Could you spare a little lunch?
YOU'LL be a little lunch if my husband, the giant, sees you!
He stole this castle and its treasures from an English family. He killed the father and sent the mother and boy packing.
YOU are that boy! If you want this place back, you must first take his coins, then his magic goose, and finally his singing harp!
Ulp-I'd rather have some lunch.
FEE! FI! FO! FUM!
Hush! That's my husband singing-hide quickly!
Th-that's singing?
I SMELL THE BLOOD OF AN ENG-LISHMAN!
IF HE'S ALIVE OR IF HE'S DEAD, I'LL USE HIS BONES TO GRIND MY BREAD!
Just stack your coins dear. Here comes lunch.
After eating, the giant fell asleep.
ZZZZZZZZZZZZZ
Now's my chance.
Oh boy! Wait 'til Mom sees this.
MOM! WE'RE RICH!
Oh, Jack!

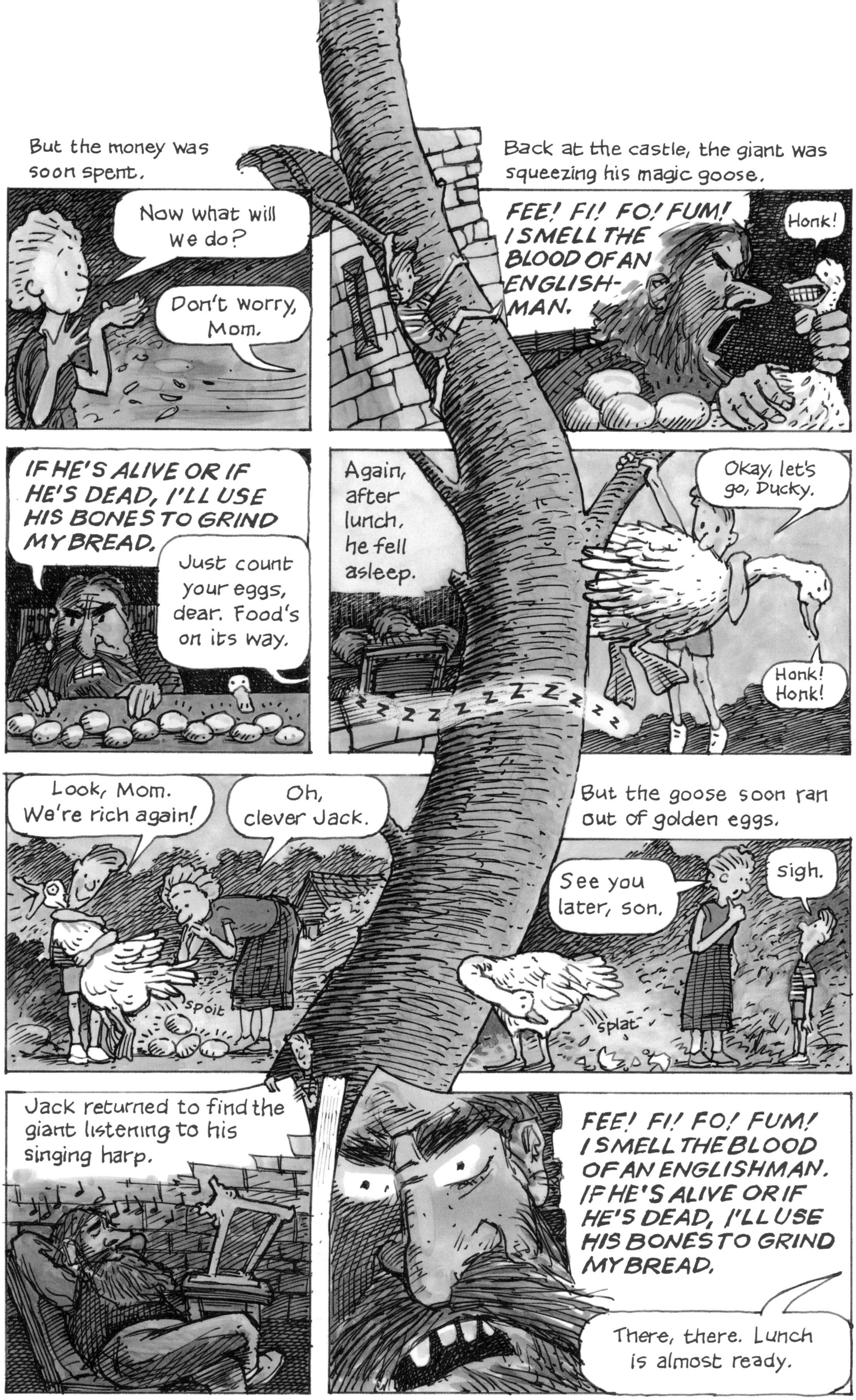
But the money was soon spent.
Now what will we do?
Don't worry, Mom.
Back at the castle, the giant was squeezing his magic goose.
FEE! FI! FO! FUM! I SMELL THE BLOOD OF AN ENGLISH-MAN.
Honk!
IF HE'S ALIVE OR IF HE'S DEAD, I'LL USE HIS BONES TO GRIND MY BREAD.
Just count your eggs, dear. Food's on its way.
Again, after lunch, he fell asleep.
Okay, let's go, Ducky.
Honk! Honk!
Look, Mom. We're rich again!
Oh, clever Jack.
spoit
But the goose soon ran out of golden eggs.
See you later, son.
sigh.
splat
Jack returned to find the giant listening to his singing harp.
FEE! FI! FO! FUM! I SMELL THE BLOOD OF AN ENGLISHMAN. IF HE'S ALIVE OR IF HE'S DEAD, I'LL USE HIS BONES TO GRIND MY BREAD.
There, there. Lunch is almost ready.

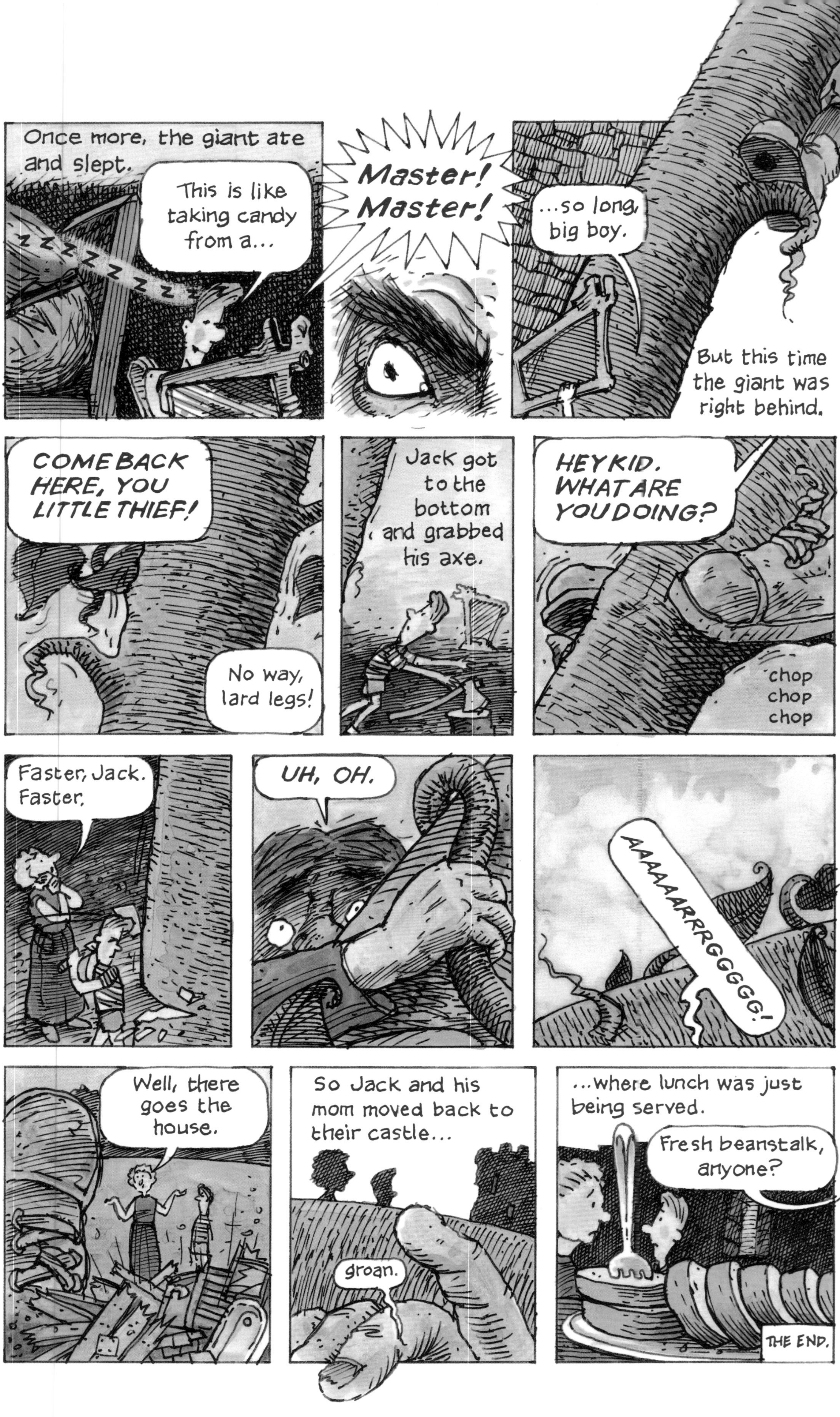
Once more, the giant ate and slept.
This is like taking candy from a...
Master! Master!
...so long, big boy.
But this time the giant was right behind.
COME BACK HERE, YOU LITTLE THIEF!
No way, lard legs!
Jack got to the bottom and grabbed his axe.
HEY KID. WHAT ARE YOU DOING?
chop chop chop
Faster, Jack. Faster.
UH, OH.
AAAAAARRRGGGGG!
Well, there goes the house.
So Jack and his mom moved back to their castle...
groan.
...where lunch was just being served.
Fresh beanstalk, anyone?
THE END.

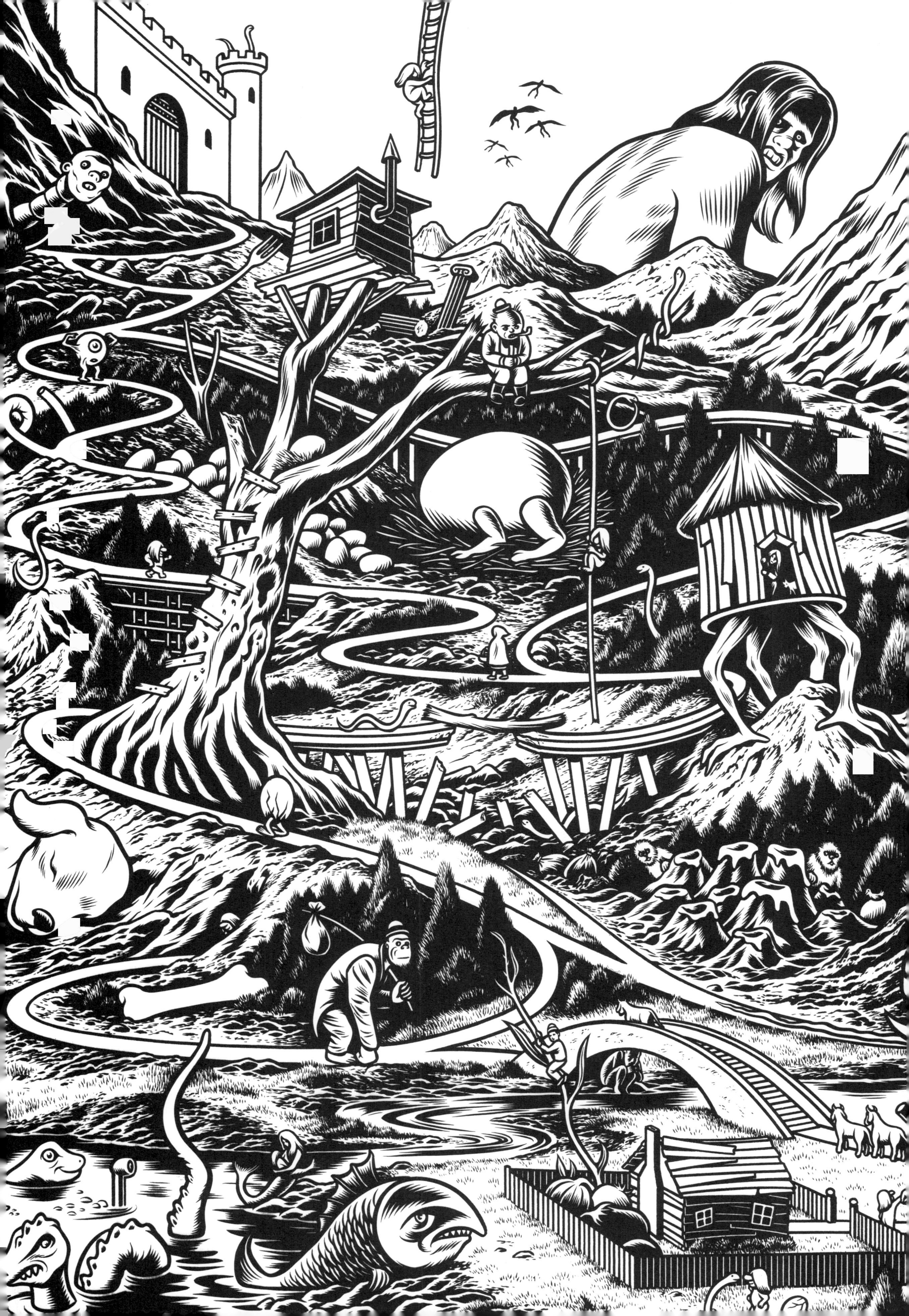

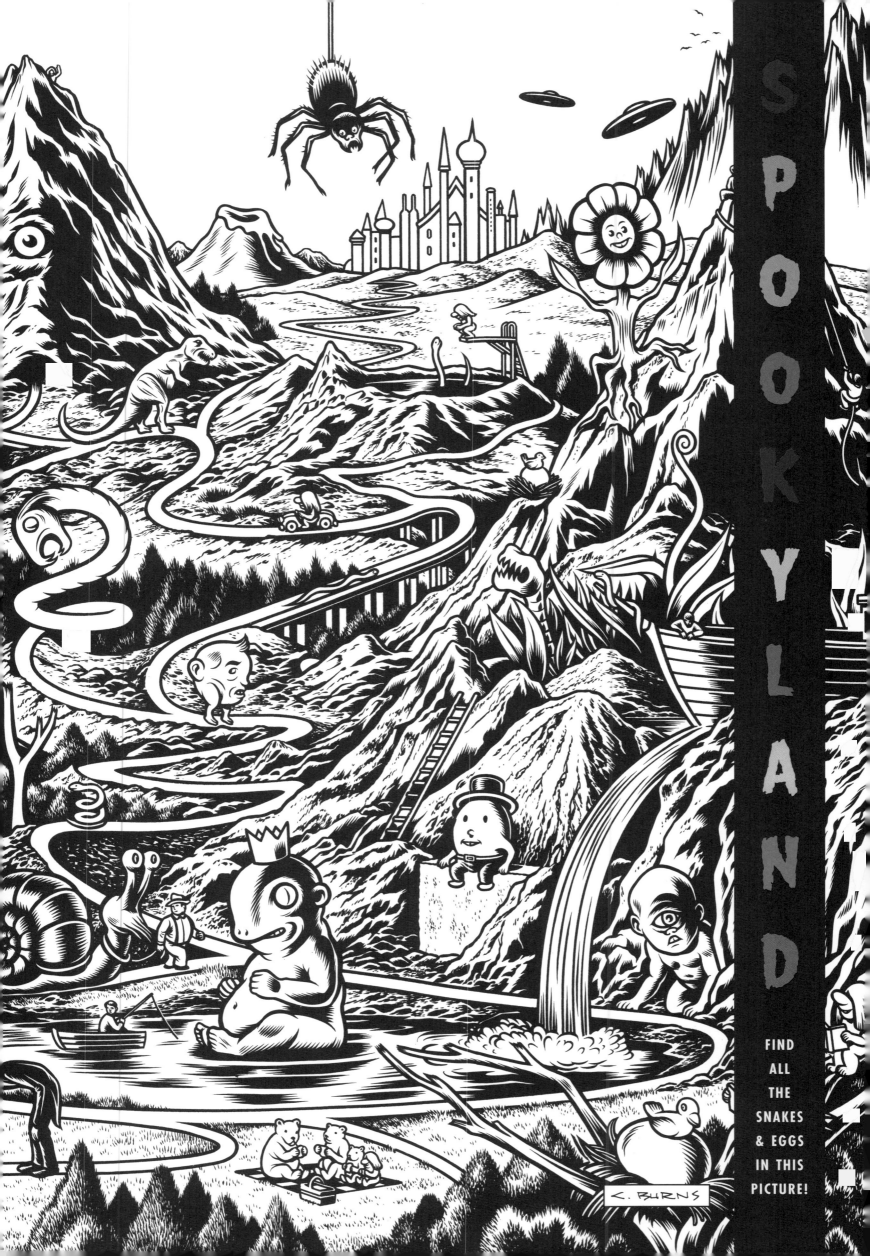

FIND
ALL
THE
SNAKES
& EGGS
IN THIS
PICTURE!

C. BURNS

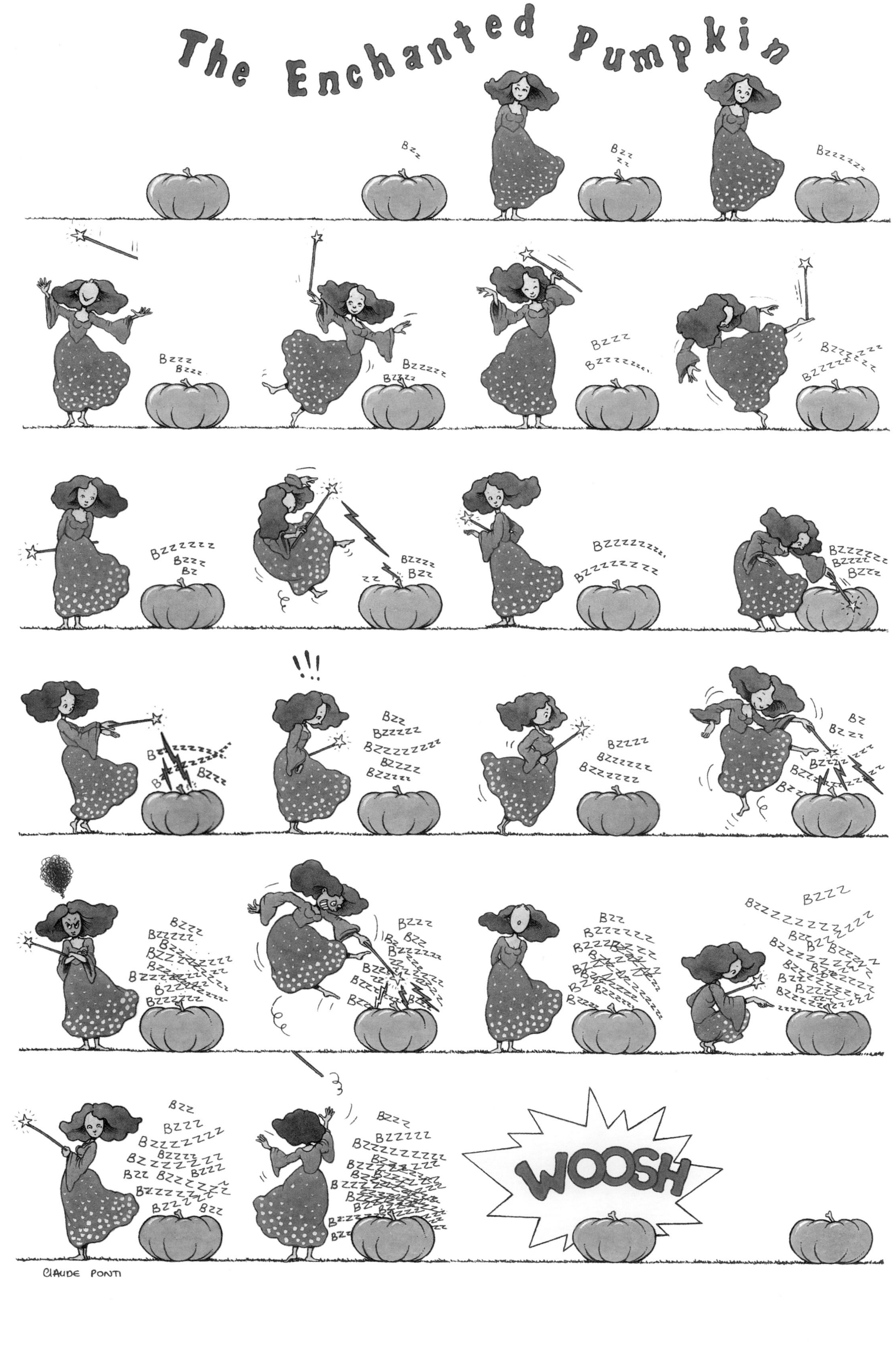
The Enchanted Pumpkin
Bzz
Bzz
Bzzzzzz
Bzzz
Bzzz
Bzzzzz
Bzzzz
Bzzz
Bzzzzzzz
Bzzzzzz
Bzzzzzz
Bzzzzzz
Bzzz
Bz
Bzzzz
Bzz
Bzzzzzzzz
Bzzzzzzzz
Bzzzzzzz
Bzzzz
Bzzz
!!!
Bzz
Bzzzzz
Bzzzzzzzz
Bzzzz
Bzzzzz
Bzzzz
Bzzzzzz
Bzzzzzz
Bz
WOOSH

CLAUDE PONTI

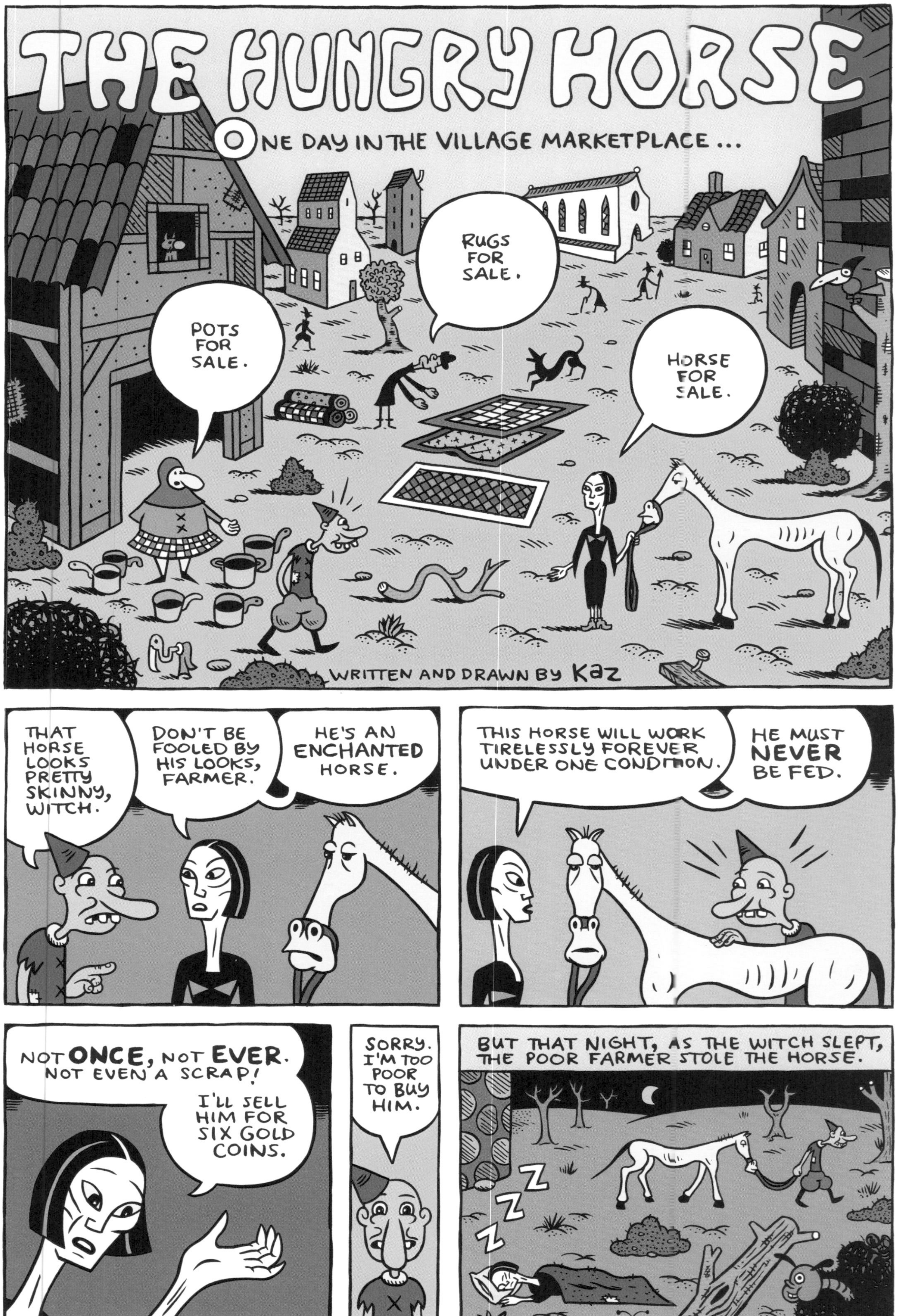
THE HUNGRY HORSE
ONE DAY IN THE VILLAGE MARKETPLACE ...
POTS FOR SALE.
RUGS FOR SALE.
HORSE FOR SALE.
WRITTEN AND DRAWN BY Kaz
THAT HORSE LOOKS PRETTY SKINNY, WITCH.
DON'T BE FOOLED BY HIS LOOKS, FARMER.
HE'S AN ENCHANTED HORSE.
THIS HORSE WILL WORK TIRELESSLY FOREVER UNDER ONE CONDITION.
HE MUST NEVER BE FED.
NOT ONCE, NOT EVER. NOT EVEN A SCRAP!
I'LL SELL HIM FOR SIX GOLD COINS.
SORRY. I'M TOO POOR TO BUY HIM.
BUT THAT NIGHT, AS THE WITCH SLEPT, THE POOR FARMER STOLE THE HORSE.
ZZZZ

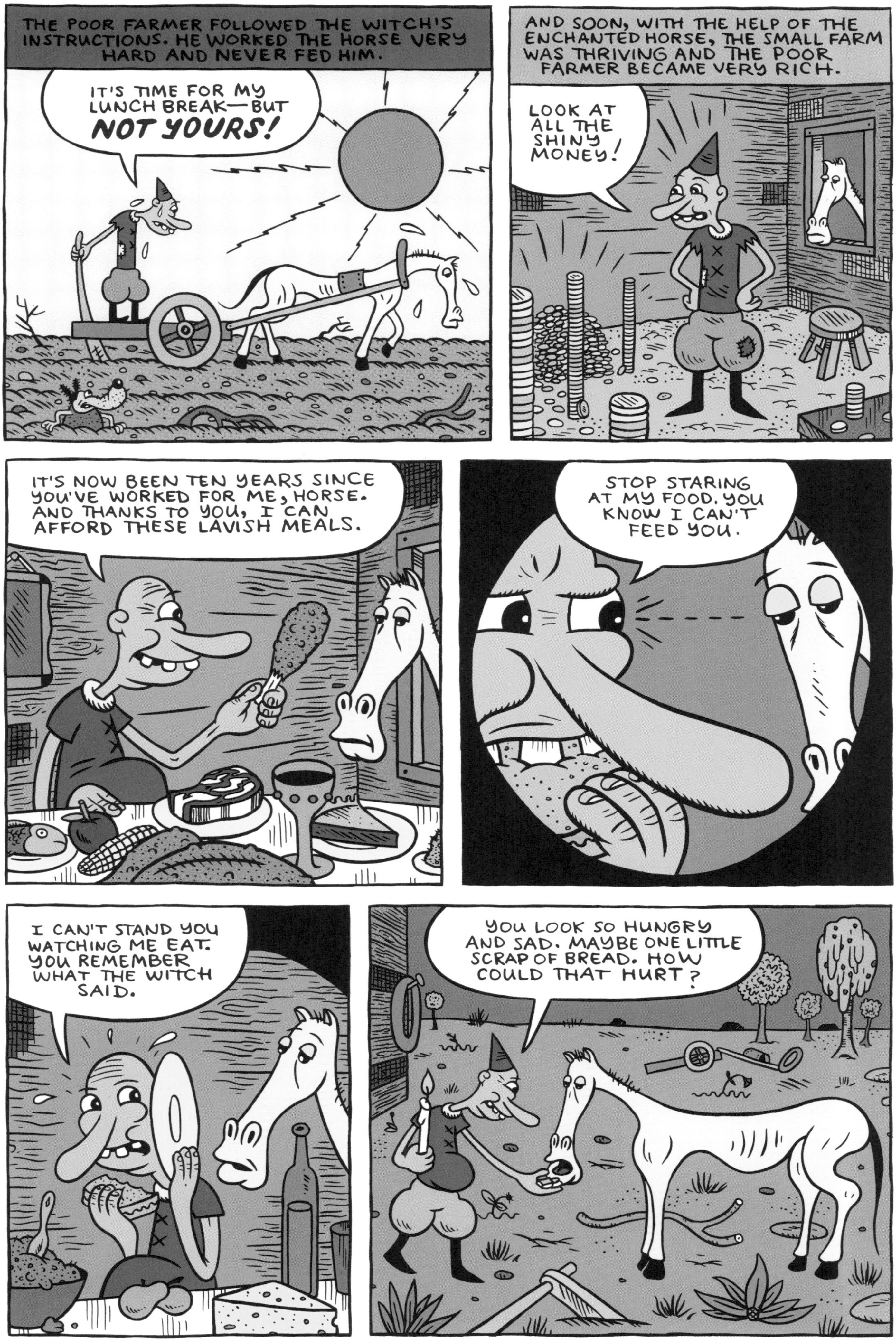
THE POOR FARMER FOLLOWED THE WITCH'S INSTRUCTIONS. HE WORKED THE HORSE VERY HARD AND NEVER FED HIM.
IT'S TIME FOR MY LUNCH BREAK—BUT NOT YOURS!
AND SOON, WITH THE HELP OF THE ENCHANTED HORSE, THE SMALL FARM WAS THRIVING AND THE POOR FARMER BECAME VERY RICH.
LOOK AT ALL THE SHINY MONEY!
IT'S NOW BEEN TEN YEARS SINCE YOU'VE WORKED FOR ME, HORSE. AND THANKS TO YOU, I CAN AFFORD THESE LAVISH MEALS.
STOP STARING AT MY FOOD. YOU KNOW I CAN'T FEED YOU.
I CAN'T STAND YOU WATCHING ME EAT. YOU REMEMBER WHAT THE WITCH SAID.
YOU LOOK SO HUNGRY AND SAD. MAYBE ONE LITTLE SCRAP OF BREAD. HOW COULD THAT HURT?

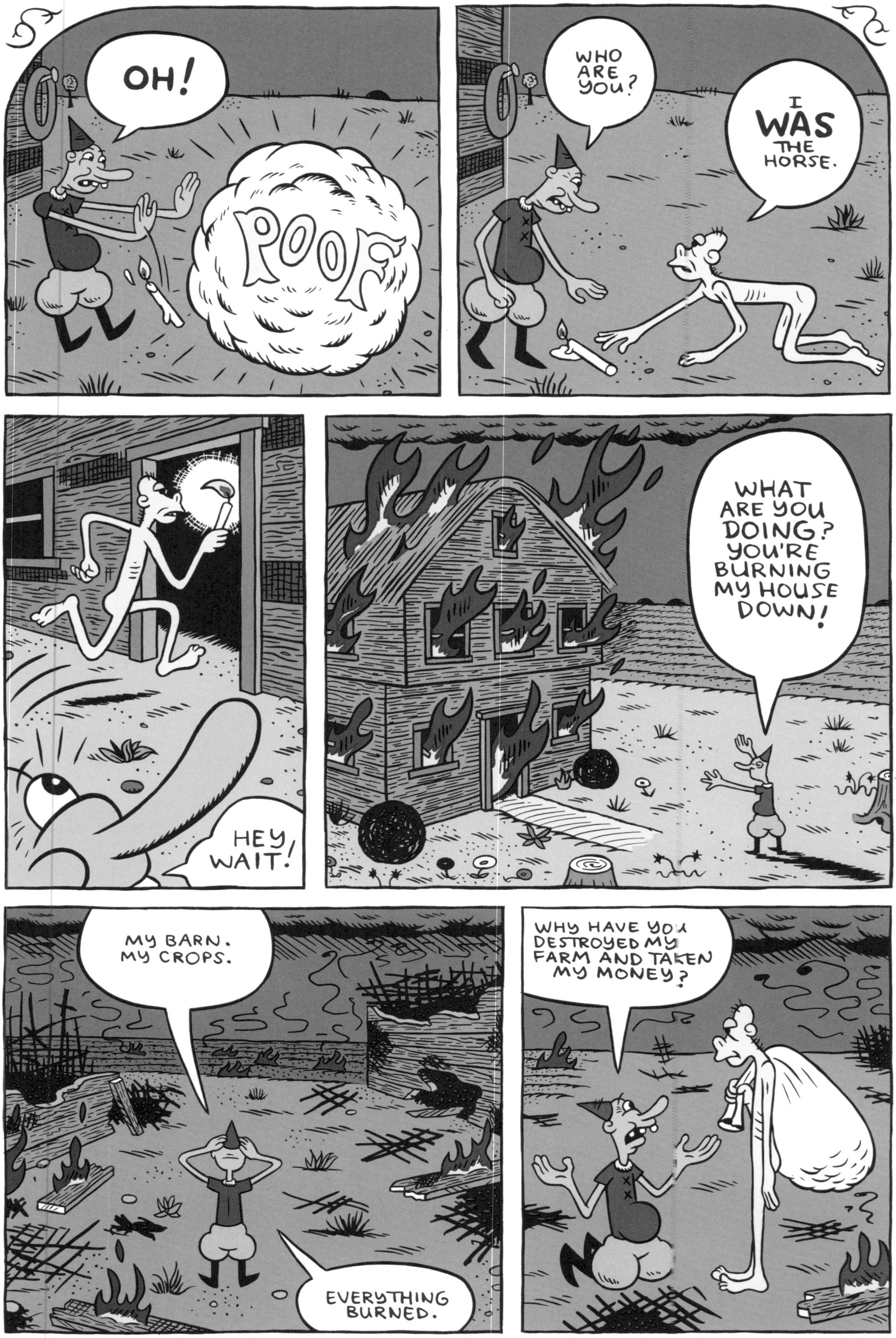
OH!
POOF
WHO ARE YOU?
I WAS THE HORSE.
HEY, WAIT!
WHAT ARE YOU DOING? YOU'RE BURNING MY HOUSE DOWN!
MY BARN. MY CROPS.
EVERYTHING BURNED.
WHY HAVE YOU DESTROYED MY FARM AND TAKEN MY MONEY?

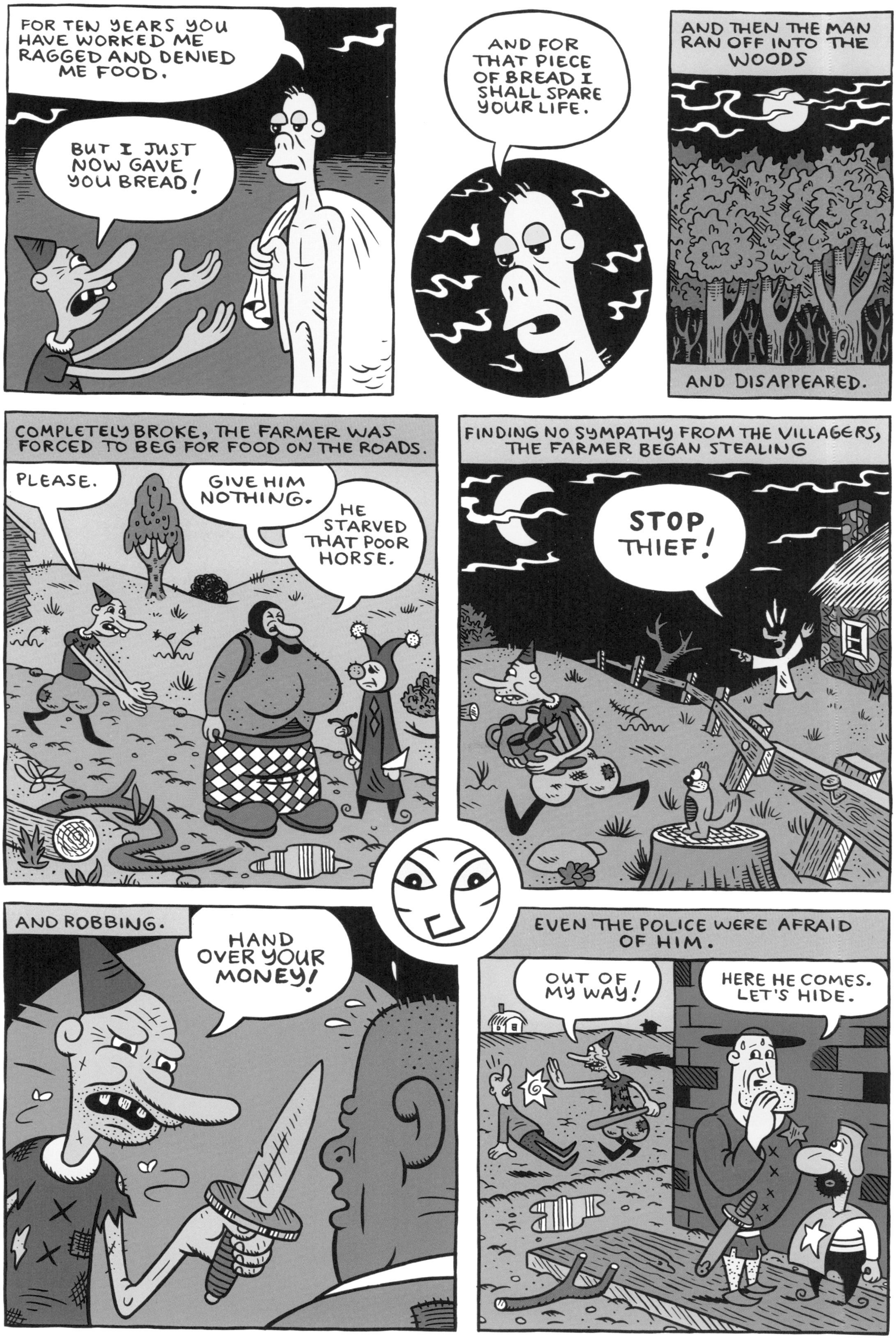
FOR TEN YEARS YOU HAVE WORKED ME RAGGED AND DENIED ME FOOD.
BUT I JUST NOW GAVE YOU BREAD!
AND FOR THAT PIECE OF BREAD I SHALL SPARE YOUR LIFE.
AND THEN THE MAN RAN OFF INTO THE WOODS
AND DISAPPEARED.
COMPLETELY BROKE, THE FARMER WAS FORCED TO BEG FOR FOOD ON THE ROADS.
PLEASE.
GIVE HIM NOTHING.
HE STARVED THAT POOR HORSE.
FINDING NO SYMPATHY FROM THE VILLAGERS, THE FARMER BEGAN STEALING
STOP THIEF!
AND ROBBING.
HAND OVER YOUR MONEY!
EVEN THE POLICE WERE AFRAID OF HIM.
OUT OF MY WAY!
HERE HE COMES. LET'S HIDE.

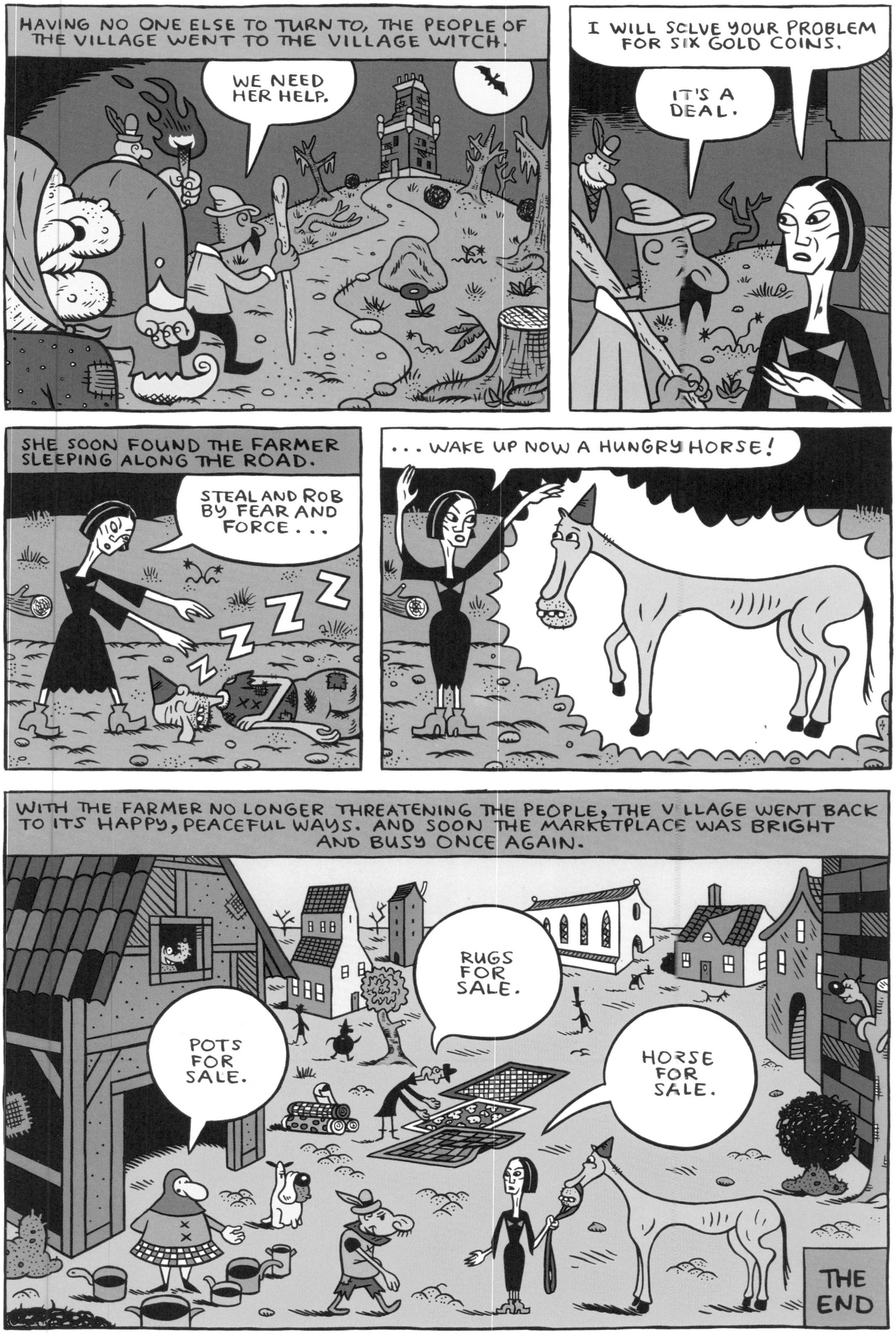
HAVING NO ONE ELSE TO TURN TO, THE PEOPLE OF THE VILLAGE WENT TO THE VILLAGE WITCH.
WE NEED HER HELP.
I WILL SOLVE YOUR PROBLEM FOR SIX GOLD COINS.
IT'S A DEAL.
SHE SOON FOUND THE FARMER SLEEPING ALONG THE ROAD.
STEAL AND ROB BY FEAR AND FORCE . . .
ZZZZZ
. . . WAKE UP NOW A HUNGRY HORSE!
WITH THE FARMER NO LONGER THREATENING THE PEOPLE, THE V LLAGE WENT BACK TO ITS HAPPY, PEACEFUL WAYS. AND SOON THE MARKETPLACE WAS BRIGHT AND BUSY ONCE AGAIN.
RUGS FOR SALE.
POTS FOR SALE.
HORSE FOR SALE.
THE END

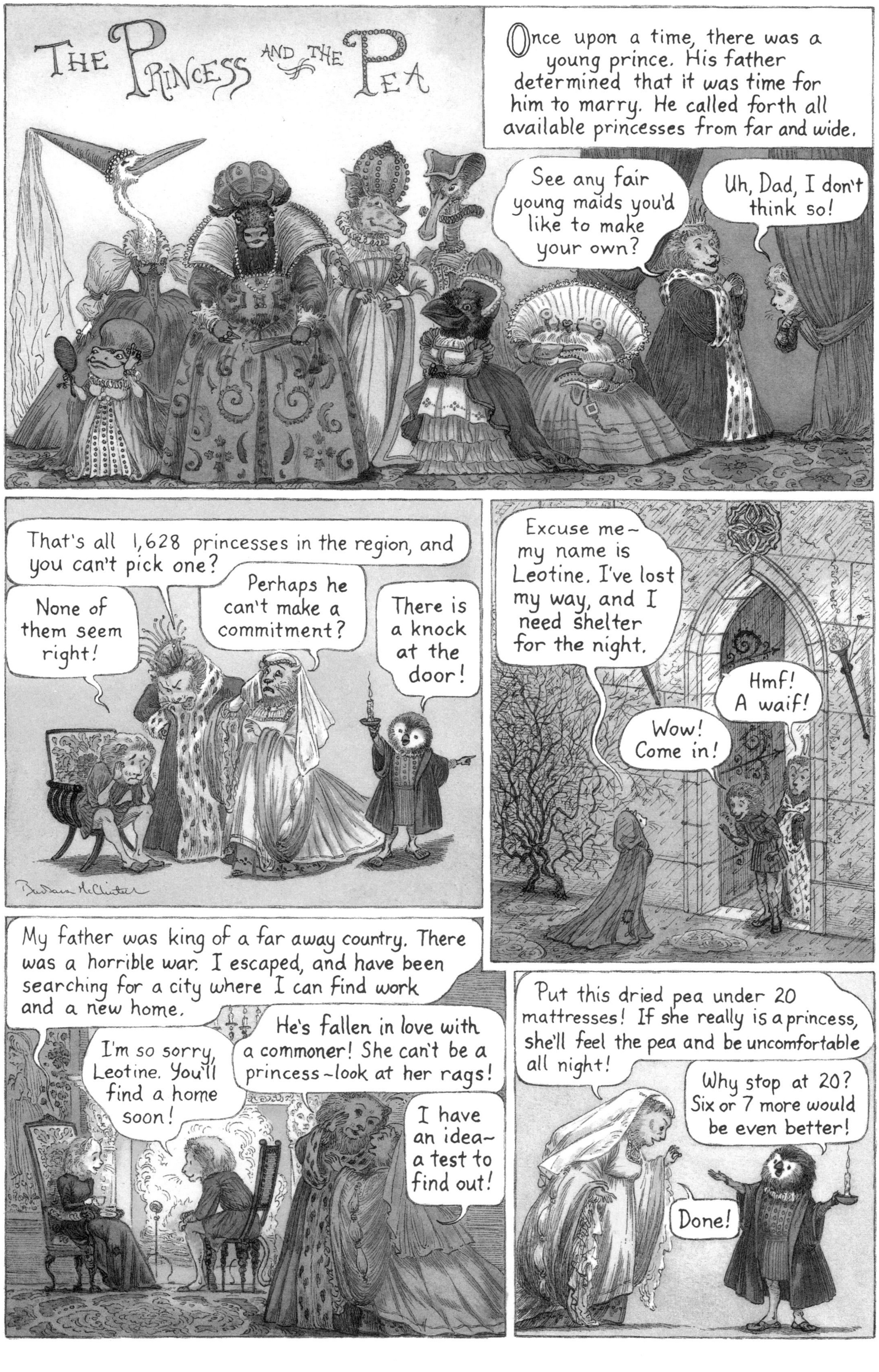
The Princess and the Pea
Once upon a time, there was a young prince. His father determined that it was time for him to marry. He called forth all available princesses from far and wide.
See any fair young maids you'd like to make your own?
Uh, Dad, I don't think so!
That's all 1,628 princesses in the region, and you can't pick one?
None of them seem right!
Perhaps he can't make a commitment?
There is a knock at the door!
Excuse me– my name is Leotine. I've lost my way, and I need shelter for the night.
Hmf! A waif!
Wow! Come in!
My father was king of a far away country. There was a horrible war. I escaped, and have been searching for a city where I can find work and a new home.
I'm so sorry, Leotine. You'll find a home soon!
He's fallen in love with a commoner! She can't be a princess–look at her rags!
I have an idea– a test to find out!
Put this dried pea under 20 mattresses! If she really is a princess, she'll feel the pea and be uncomfortable all night!
Why stop at 20? Six or 7 more would be even better!
Done!

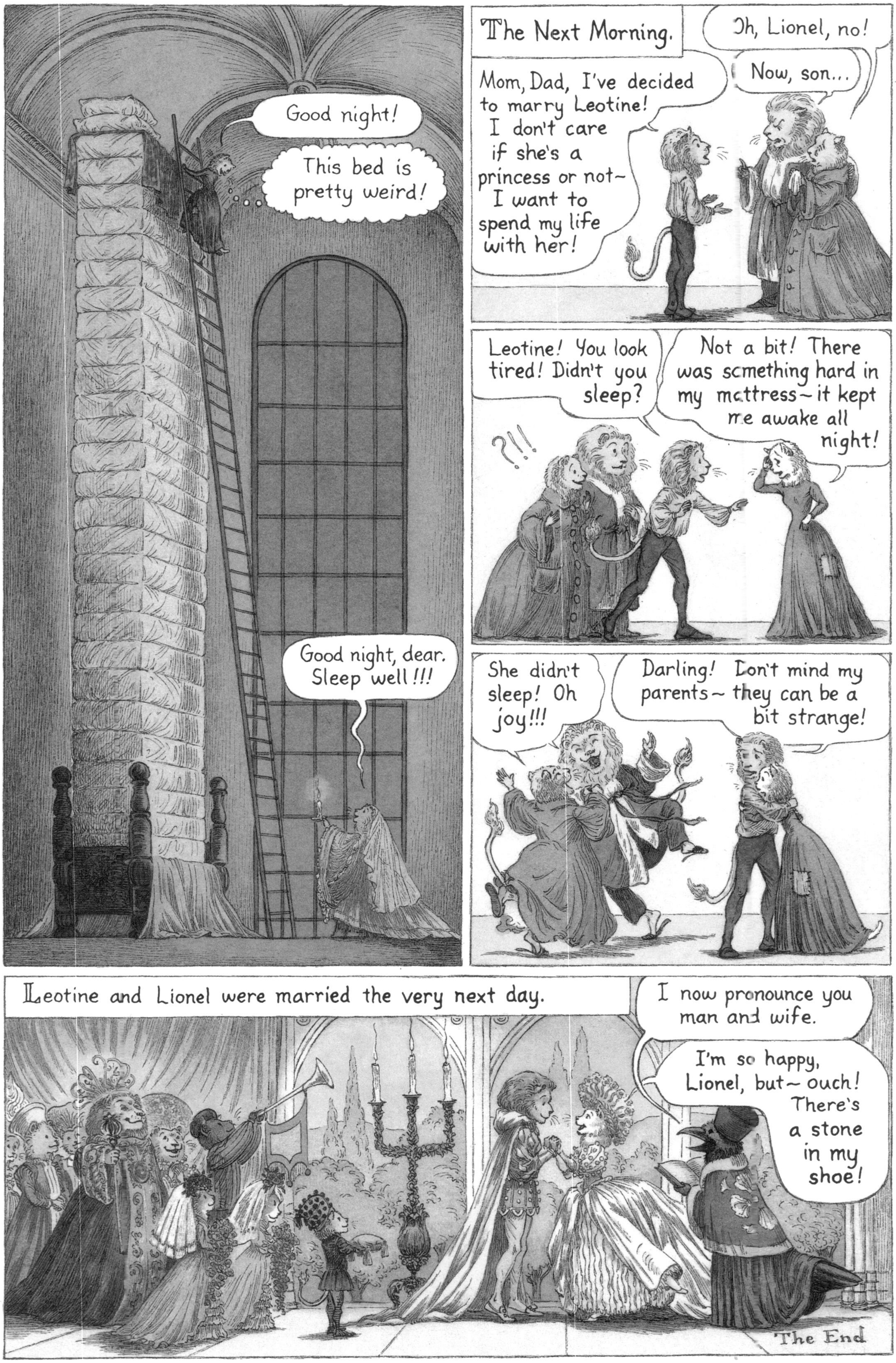
Good night!
This bed is pretty weird!
Good night, dear. Sleep well!!!
The Next Morning.
Mom, Dad, I've decided to marry Leotine! I don't care if she's a princess or not~ I want to spend my life with her!
Oh, Lionel, no!
Now, son...
Leotine! You look tired! Didn't you sleep?
Not a bit! There was something hard in my mattress~ it kept me awake all night!
?!!
She didn't sleep! Oh joy!!!
Darling! Don't mind my parents~ they can be a bit strange!
Leotine and Lionel were married the very next day.
I now pronounce you man and wife.
I'm so happy, Lionel, but~ ouch! There's a stone in my shoe!
The End

CONTRIBUTOR NOTES

ART SPIEGELMAN, who also painted the covers, wrote and drew *Prince Rooster* because he "wanted to find a fairy tale with no magic, except the magic of good stories." He is the Pulitzer Prize-winning author of *MAUS: A Survivor's Tale*, an account of his parents' experiences in the Holocaust, as well as a children's book, *Open Me... I'm a Dog!* He is a staff writer and artist for *The New Yorker*. Born in Sweden, Art now lives in Manhattan with his wife and co-editor, Françoise Mouly, and their two children, Nadja, 13, and Dashiell, 8. FRANÇOISE MOULY, born and raised in Paris, France, studied architecture at the Beaux Arts before coming to the U.S. at the age of 19. Beginning in 1980, she was the publisher, co-founder, and co-editor, with Art Spiegelman, of *RAW Magazine*, a comics anthology for adults. Françoise has been the art editor of *The New Yorker* since 1993.

WILLIAM JOYCE is the creator of numerous children's books, including *Dinosaur Bob* and *Santa Calls*, as well as the television series *Rolie Polie Olie*. He was born in Shreveport, LA, where he now lives with his wife, their two children, and two pets: a dog and a cat. Having children made Bill think about eggs, Humpty Dumpty, and *Humpty Trouble*. He is currently working with Disney to bring *Dinosaur Bob* to animated life.

EVER MEULEN lives in Brussels with his wife and four cats. His grown-up son is now a computer wizard who helps Ever with the digitizing of his graphic work, such as *A Knight to Remember*. Ever is an internationally recognized illustrator and designer whose work has been featured in *The New Yorker* and many other publications. Recently, he was asked to do a drawing as a gift for the wedding of Prince Philip of Belgium.

DANIEL CLOWES, born in Chicago, lives with his wife, Erika, and their pet snake in Berkeley, CA. His past work includes the ongoing comic book *Eightball*. This version of *The Sleeping Beauty* is based upon the original 17th-century telling by Charles Perrault. This year will see the release of a new graphic novel by Dan, *David Boring*, and in 2001, a movie based on his work, *Ghost World*, will come out.

JOOST SWARTE, like the characters in *The Leafless Tree*, lives in Haarlem, the Netherlands, a city which has adopted the symbol of a leafless tree. He is married and has three daughters and two cats. Among his many past projects are a series of comics for children and Dutch postage stamps. Joost is now working on a children's book and the architectural design of a theater in Haarlem that will open in 2002.

BRUCE McCALL, of *What's Wrong with This Picture?*, lives in Manhattan with his wife, their daughter, Amanda, and a Himalayan cat. A regular contributor to *The New Yorker* and *Vanity Fair*, Bruce has had exhibitions of his work in Paris and New York. He is the author of two books: *Zany Afternoons*, an illustrated book of humor, and *Thin Ice*, a memoir. Bruce is currently at work on two more illustrated humor books.

DAVID MAZZUCCHELLI recently received a grant to live and work in Japan for six months, where he can learn more about the inspiration for *The Fisherman and the Sea Princess*, the character Urashima Tarō. His work has been published by *Nickelodeon Magazine* and DC Comics and in his own self-published magazine, *Rubber Blanket*. Currently working on an original graphic novel, David lives in Manhattan.

LORENZO MATTOTTI, the artist behind *The Two Hunchbacks*, was born in Italy but now lives in Paris with Rina, their two children, a pet fish, a giant snail, and a rabbit. Lorenzo has published two graphic novels for adults in the U.S.: *Murmur* and *Fires*. In Europe, he has created acclaimed magazine and fashion illustrations, as well as many books for children and adults. Currently he is working on an animated film of *Pinocchio*.

WALT KELLY (1913-1973) was the creator of *Pogo*, a comic strip admired by adults and kids alike for its sophisticated political satires clothed in a deceptively pretty style. Kelly perfected this technique during his years as an animator for Walt Disney, most notably on the film *Fantasia*. In the 1940s he produced stories for *Fairy Tale Parade*, in which *The Gingerbread Man* was published, and *Animal Comics*, where *Pogo* first appeared.

HARRY BLISS read the old English folktale *The Baker's Daughter* to his six year-old son, Alexander, who has since resolved to be kind, for fear of being turned into an owl. Currently at work on writing and illustrating children's books, Harry is a cartoonist for *Archeology Magazine* and a staff artist at *The New Yorker*. Born in Rochester, NY, Harry now lives in Burlington, VT, with Alexander and their pet turtle, Sara.

J. OTTO SEIBOLD's work has appeared in numerous magazines and his animation has been featured on MTV. He is the creator, with his wife Vivian Walsh, of children's books, including *Monkey Business, Mr. Lunch Takes a Plane Ride*, and *Olive, the Other Reindeer*, which became a one-hour television show. *Can You Find the Twins?* was made in San Francisco, CA, where J. Otto and Vivian live with their three good-looking kids.

DAVID MACAULAY is the creator behind such books as *Cathedral* and *The Way Things Work*. Born in England, David has lived in America for most of his life. He now resides in Rhode Island with his wife, Ruthie, and their daughter and son. Upcoming work includes a PBS documentary and an accompanying book. *Jack and the Beanstalk* is David's first comic; he thought it was a fun challenge in play and pictures.

CHARLES BURNS, who drew *Spookyland*, was born in Washington, DC, and now lives in Philadelphia with his wife, Susan, and their two daughters. He is the creator of the ongoing comic book *Black Hole*, as well as the illustrator behind memorable images for magazines such as *Time* and *Rolling Stone*. This year will see the completion of a four-volume collection of his comics work, to be published by Fantagraphics.

CLAUDE PONTI, who was born in northern France, lives in Paris with his wife, his daughter Adèle, and a cat. He is the creator of over fifty very popular children's books, all published in Europe. About his story Claude told us, "One day a little fairy came to my table. 'What is your story?' asked my drawing pen. 'I have a problem with a pumpkin!' And the pumpkin came to my table and said 'buzzzz.' What could I do?"

KAZ was born in Hoboken, NJ, and now lives in Manhattan. He is the creator of *Underworld*, a weekly comic strip for adults, which has been collected in three books published by Fantagraphics. Kaz is also a regular contributor to *Nickelodeon Magazine*. He claims that *The Hungry Horse*, actually a variation on a story of Estonian descent, was told to him at a racetrack by a one-armed gypsy horse doctor.

BARBARA McCLINTOCK grew up in Flemington, NJ and North Dakota. As a first grader, her sister played the princess in the musical version of *The Princess and the Pea*. Barbara is the award-winning creator of such children's books as *Animal Fables from Aesop, The Heartaches of a French Cat*, and *The Battle of Luke and Longnose*. She now lives in New Canaan, CT, with her son, Larson, and their pets: a cat and a fish.

CHRIS WARE, the creator of *The Fairy Tale Road Rage Game*, was never a child and always hated fairy tales. Born in Nebraska, he now resides in Chicago with his wife, Marnie, and their three cats. Chris produces the award-winning ongoing comic books for adults, *The Acme Novelty Library*, some of which have been collected in this year's book from Pantheon, *Jimmy Corrigan, The Smartest Kid on Earth*.

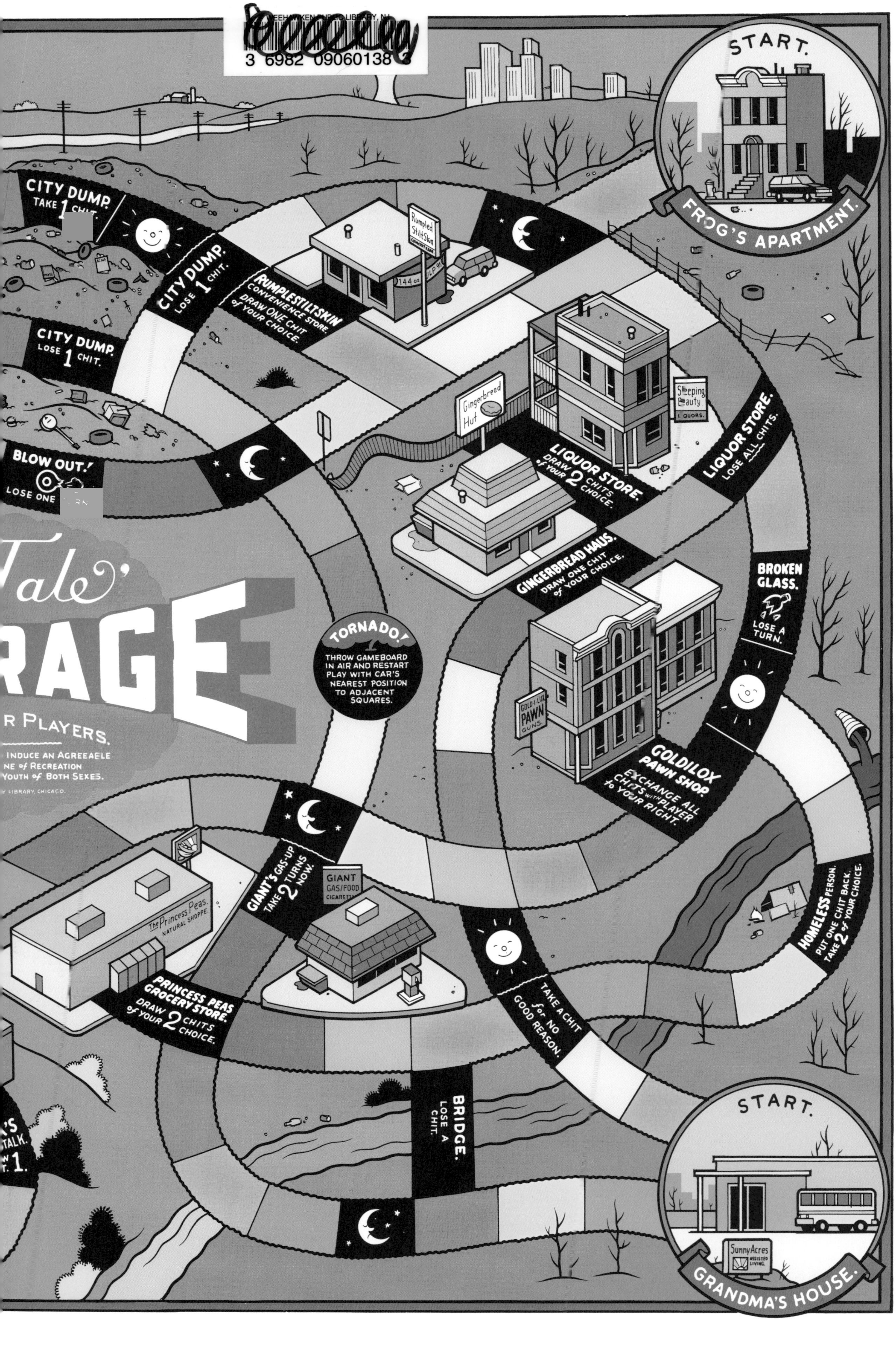
START.
FROG'S APARTMENT.
CITY DUMP. TAKE 1 CHIT.
CITY DUMP. LOSE 1 CHIT.
RUMPLESTILTSKIN CONVENIENCE STORE. DRAW ONE CHIT of YOUR CHOICE.
Rumpled StiltSkin
CITY DUMP. LOSE 1 CHIT.
Gingerbread Hut
Sleeping Beauty LIQUORS
LIQUOR STORE. DRAW 2 CHITS of YOUR CHOICE.
LIQUOR STORE. LOSE ALL CHITS.
BLOW OUT!
LOSE ONE
GINGERBREAD HAUS. DRAW ONE CHIT of YOUR CHOICE.
BROKEN GLASS. LOSE A TURN.
Tale'
RAGE
R PLAYERS.
INDUCE AN AGREEAELE
NE of RECREATION
YOUTH of BOTH SEXES.
W LIBRARY, CHICAGO.
TORNADO! THROW GAMEBOARD IN AIR AND RESTART PLAY WITH CAR'S NEAREST POSITION TO ADJACENT SQUARES.
GOLD-I-LUX PAWN GUNS
GOLDILOX PAWN SHOP. EXCHANGE ALL CHITS with PLAYER to YOUR RIGHT.
GIANT'S GAS-UP TAKE 2 TURNS NOW.
GIANT GAS/FOOD CIGARETTES
The Princess Peas. NATURAL SHOPPE.
PRINCESS PEAS GROCERY STORE. DRAW 2 CHITS of YOUR CHOICE.
TAKE A CHIT for NO GOOD REASON.
HOMELESS PERSON. PUT ONE CHIT BACK. TAKE 2 of YOUR CHOICE.
BRIDGE. LOSE A CHIT.
'S
TALK.
W
T. 1.
START.
GRANDMA'S HOUSE.
SunnyAcres ASSISTED LIVING.